C0-CFJ-921

# IF YOU PLAY WITH FIRE

6/5/09
To Sam —

# IF
# YOU PLAY WITH
# FIRE

*Eugene L. Welischar*

Brothers Always

Gene Welesh

**ADVOCATE HOUSE**
SARASOTA, FL

Copyright © 2009 by A Cappela Publishing
All rights reserved.

No part of this book may be reproduced or transmitted in any form, by any means electronic
or mechanical, including photocopying, recording, or any information storage and retrieval
system now known or to be invented without permission in writing from the author, except
by a reviewer who wishes to quote passages in connection with a review written in a
magazine, newspaper, or broadcast.

For information regarding permissions, write to:
A Cappela Publishing
913 Tennessee Lane
Sarasota FL 34234

LIBRARY OF CONGRESS CATALOGING-IN-PUBLICATION DATA:
Welischar, Eugene L.
If You Play With Fire / Eugene L. Welischar. — 1st ed.
p.   cm.
1. Fiction—Adult.  2. Firefighting—New York City—Arson.
Government—NYC—CIA—FBI.

First Edition

*Design by Carol Tornatore*

Printed in Canada

# DEDICATION

This book is dedicated to Greg Stajk, who was my "probie," and the ten firemen of Ladder 13 and Engine 22 who gave their lives at the World Trade Center on Sept. 11, 2001. Most of these men came after I had left this firehouse, though I knew many of them from fire department functions.

This book is also dedicated to all who lost their lives on 9/11 — including the uniformed services, the construction and Red Cross workers and the men and women who gave their all on "the pile."

Importantly, this book recognizes the people who worked at the World Trade Center, who represented the cream of our country in the prime of their lives and to the many heroes and their untold stories. I will never forget them and their surviving families.

This dedication would be incomplete without mention of Ellen, the love of my life, without whom I could never have completed this book, and to my daughter Annie, whose creativity was so helpful, particularly in the outstanding-dynamic design of the front cover.

I went to Patrika Vaughn's seminar on How to Write Your Own Life Story and was impressed, so I made an appointment with her. After discussing my project, I was convinced that she was the editor I needed—and she proved me right.

*This photo of Greg Stajk with Victor the Constrictor was taken 20 years before Greg was killed at the World Trade Center on 9/11, along with the many other service people who gave their lives that day.*

# OUT OF MY LIFE AND THOUGHT

## Albert Schweitzer

*"Only a person who can find a value in every sort of activity and devote himself to each one with full conscientiousness of duty, has the inward right to take as his object some extraordinary activity instead of that which naturally falls to his lot. Only a person who feels his preference to be a matter of course, not something out of the ordinary, and who has no thought of heroism, but just recognizes a duty undertaken with sober enthusiasm, is capable of becoming a spiritual adventurer such as the world needs."*

# FOREWORD

With this book, based in the tumultuous 1960s and 70s, I try to capture the essence of the complete unsung fireman. His story begins the day he walks into the firehouse for the first time as a probie — a day he will never forget. Wide eyed, nervous and excited each new "probie" wants to add to and become part of the heritage he has heard so much about. He is consumed with thoughts of his first fire — what it will be like, whether he can make the grade. He will recognize the concern and droll humor of his new "brothers," and he will come to understand their regard and efforts for his welfare. He will soon become one with a job he will love for the rest of his life.

For all the camaraderie that existed back in the 1960s and 70s, however, there were also drawbacks to this closeness of the brotherhood. With second jobs to supplement incomes plus the additional commitments required by their home-away-from-home firehouse's extraordinary work load, some firemen had problems with their home lives and marriages. Some wives felt that they had to play second fiddle to the "brotherhood" and to the fire department in general. Separations and divorces were byproducts of the stresses and strains of the job in this era. The brotherhood survived it.

Then and now, newly assigned officers in a fire department company look for the informal leaders in the group, the ones that shape the character of the company. In addition to their unquestioned duty and devotion to save lives and properties, it is the incidental things these informal leaders do on a daily basis to make the men Complete Firemen. They show comradeship by doing menial jobs such as cooking, cleaning and maintenance of the fire house, the supplying of food for company dances, picnics and the frequent memorial services. This Complete Fireman is the backbone of the fire service, the mortar and bricks that keep it all together. In this book I have interspersed brief looks into the makeup of the Fire Department and its members, with a few vignettes that show their devotion to their calling and their many acts of compassion for the public they serve.

# PRELUDE

*Slightly past midnight, Danny O (La Torcia to his peers) slips a key into the door and silently enters the empty apartment. He looks for an area where his fire will not be discovered too quickly. He uses no accelerant: too easily detected.*

*He selects his spot and sets the stage: spoon, matches, syringe and blanket — heroin users' tools — and carefully places a few magazines and newspapers around the discarded furniture he has strewn around the blanket. This will be his ignition area, a setting to throw off arson investigators.*

*Danny O has studied the chemistry of fire and knows that objects do not burn; it is the gases given off by the fire that burn as the objects are heated. The many layers of oil-based paints in the building's apartments also give off gases when heated, very toxic gases.*

*He has selected an area near an interior light shaft, away from the entrance and front windows of the apartment which will be left slightly open to give the fire needed oxygen. This way the smoke will enter the shaft, probably remaining undetected until the fire has a good hold. His night timing is good. The few remaining tenants are old and go to bed early. He crumples several sheets of newspapers and sets the fire on the blanket.*

*Danny O quickly leaves the apartment, making sure the door stays unlocked. He stealthily descends the stairs to the street and heads outside to watch the drama unfold.*

*He enters the building across the street and, using one of his many lock openers on the vestibule door, he heads to the roof. Danny O knows that by law the bulkhead door can never be locked from the inside, so his access to the roof is unimpeded. He will have a perfect view of the fire.*

*In an obscure area he awaits the arrival of the fire department.*

*He is well paid for his work of scaring tenants into moving. He is the last resort of impatient property owners, owners who first offer cash to entice tenants to leave. That failing, new heartless supers are installed to harass the tenants by withholding heat or hot water, performing unnecessary noisy repairs at odd hours and various other irritants. Danny O has had a lot of work from the new builders who want fast access to the space occupied by these old buildings for their business ventures.*

*Time passes slowly for Danny O. He crouches on the roof and worries that too much time has passed with the fire remaining undetected. Did it go out? Should he go back and check? He nervously waits. Finally he sees a slight red tint in the front windows. It has taken a good hold after all. Now he hears the wail of sirens and sees the fire trucks in the distance. By the time the fire department arrives the fire has broken out through the front windows.*

*Elated and excited, he watches their operations. As always, Danny O is impressed by the firefighters teamwork, looking like an army of ants swarming to attack the threatening interloper.*

*The firemen quickly put the fire out. Danny O furtively descends the stairs into the street and silently mingles with the crowd of onlookers who watch the rest of the firemen's actions. The silent crowd suddenly becomes agitated. A fat lady in the crowd is yelling about being burned out of her home. The crowd responds, joining in the shouting.*

*Danny O heads to the corner to hail a cab to his apartment, fifteen blocks away just below Spanish Harlem. There he will have a few stiff drinks to calm himself and assesses his performance. It's just a job.*

*He prefers that no deaths or injuries will result from the fire, but only because that could bring serious investigation. When he gets to the corner he sees an ambulance with blaring sirens entering the block. He looks back and sees a flurry of action at the fire site. He heads back to see what is happening. The fat bitch is now yelling about firemen being hurt. He waits until he sees a stretcher being carried from the building bearing a fireman whose head is bandaged and who appears to have a splint on one leg. The medics place the fireman in the ambulance. They're still working on him as the ambulance takes off. Danny O returns to the corner to hail a cab, but now he is agitated, upset by what he has seen. This will bring mass attention to his work and he worries about the coming investigation.*

*Arson, his field, has been lucrative for many reasons. He is well known in the business and connections with organized crime gets him many referrals for various types of arson jobs. One type, known as "Jewish Lightning," profits failing businesses with insurance payouts for the fire-destroyed structures. His present employer, Wainwright Management, prefers the type which scares stubborn remaining tenants into vacating their walk-up apartments. He gets* calls also from demolition companies to set fires in vacant buildings they are to tear down because this gets them an added "hazard" bonus of ten percent. Danny O has had a great run of work in New York's booming building market with no threats of being arrested or discovered — although, this new mayor is promising changes in arson enforcement and prosecution. If that comes to pass, Danny considers that it may then be time to go home to Italy, where he has stashed a lot of cash with his parents, and retire. He even has Social Security benefits that will follow him.

He came to this country from Salerno, Sicily twelve and a half years earlier at the age of 40, with a forged birth certificate that listed him as 50. He was immediately put to work for a "connected" construction company that sponsored him for a green card. An immigration lawyer was hired to expedite the procedure and in two years he received his card. He has paid into Social Security from being put on the books for many no-show jobs run by the "families" he does work for and in ten years, when in reality he will be fifty-two, he will be eligible to apply for Social Security Retirement Benefits. His mother and father, Lena and Mario who put him through School in Italy, are overwhelmed by his success. After school he just couldn't connect on anything that made money in the Old Country and so he decided to move to The Land of Opportunity.

He was not the typical Italian Immigrant. His English was good as a result of tutoring by his mother's sister, Maria, who returned to Italy after World War II, having lived in the United States for twenty years as a teacher. She always insisted that if he was to go to America he would have to know English and she became part of his education.

*He does not look, act or speak like his goombah contemporaries. He reads* The New York Times *and does not dress in handmade shoes, silk shirts, rich gabardine slacks and cashmere outer garments. He does not wear diamonds and gold. He dresses conservatively and could easily be mistaken for a white collar worker. When he goes on jobs he dresses down to plain sneakers, sweat shirt and pants and a baseball cap, none with graphic markings that could draw attention. Though he does not look like his mob associates, he is just as cruel, cunning and deadly.*

# Chapter 1

# IF YOU PLAY WITH FIRE

I T WAS SUNDAY, near midnight in Yorkville on New York's upper east side.

I'd been promoted from Lieutenant to Captain three years earlier, and was assigned to Ladder Company 13, a tower ladder located on 85th Street between Lexington and 3rd Avenue.

On this mild beautiful night in June of 1979, a person passing the firehouse with its doors wide open could view the two sleeping red giants — pumper Engine 22 and the hulking tower Ladder 13, my assigned company. Off to the left side of the firehouse entrance sat a fireman in the house watch cubicle and a little farther back was my Captain's office.

My evening reports were finished. I was looking out of my office, past the nose of the big tower ladder, watching and listening to the happy noises from the street. The locals had come back from their summer weekend and the quiet city had sprung back into life.

When I wasn't looking out the door I was watching the firehouse's pet boa constrictor, Victor the Constrictor. Victor lived in a huge fish tank. He'd been there since he was 12 inches long and had now grown to almost two feet, due to his initial diet of white mice and, recently, white rats. When the fire department photo unit came to quarters to upgrade I.D. laminated cards, Victor's picture was taken and posted on his tank.

For the past two days his next meal had been in the tank, but Victor had hardly noticed it. The rat was fretful and jerky, sensing his fate. Only when he was hungry would Victor go after the rat. One rat had been too tough and too smart and was removed from the tank because he'd been biting Victor's head. For now, Victor made no move. He was not yet bone hungry. I watched Victor's tongue slither in and out as he slowly slid toward his next meal. From a lethargic state to one lightning-like strike, he wrapped his forward body around the rat's neck. He unhinged his jaws and elongated his body as he crushed the rat with his powerful inner muscles, slowly digesting the rat. His strong gastric juices would disintegrate the rat's body in two days, bones and all. It seemed cruel, but he only killed according to the law of nature, when he was hungry. By contrast, man often killed for profit, or passion, using multiple means to accomplish his goal — including arson.

I lit a cigarette and again gazed toward the street. I craved a scotch and water but dismissed that thought, instead contemplating my assignment at Ladder Co. 13 (L13) since July, three years ago. Before that I had spent nine years at Engine Co. 218 (E218) in Brooklyn's Bushwick ghetto, carrying a superhuman work load during the traumatic years of the Vietnam War. Bushwick and other ghetto areas, with their poverty, arson for profit, crime and potential explosiveness, was strictly a young fireman's job. Approaching 45, I relished working in Yorkville and a return to normalcy. New York had gone through a fiscal crisis in 1975 but here, in 1979, there seemed to be an upward trend. Yes, my assignment to L13 in the plush rich Upper East Side was a welcomed change.

Suddenly, from the house watch cubicle, the new fire department computer jumped alive with it's warning tone: "Box 1062, First Ave and 79th Street," the house watchman announced over the intercom. "Engine 22, Ladder 13, Battalion 10, respond!'

During the past few months there had been several tenement fires on that block. Rumor had it that a hi-rise residential building was to be built where the old four story walk-up tenements now stood. Fire Marshals had been previously notified that these fires were of a suspicious nature, but the Marshal's office, decimated by the fiscal crisis, was limited to only two Fire Marshals available per day for arson investigations in all five boroughs.

The house watchman handed printouts to each officer of the fire trucks and their drivers (commonly referred to as chauffeurs) as well as the Battalion Chief's chauffeur. The printouts contained information on the street alarm box that has been pulled by a citizen: the box number, its location, and all available information,

I got into my equipment and fire gear and took my position in the cab of the Tower Ladder. Joe Moore, my chauffer, hopped in beside me.

"Where to, Cap?"

"First Ave and 79th. "We're first due."

The two sleeping giants roar into life, their brilliant red flashing lights and thunderous diesel engines consuming the apparatus garage. Chauffeur Gus Peterson (Hagar the Terrible), the driver and pump operator of E22, waved from his cab and slowly moved into the street.

The E22 crew, after holding up traffic, takes their places on the Engine and proceeds to Lexington Avenue. My Tower Ladder repeats the operation and we head toward the alarm box location. We move down Lexington to 79th, siren's blaring, then east to First Avenue. The 10th Battalion Chief's car follows.

As we approach the scene E44, the first due engine, comes on the department radio.

"E44 to Manhattan."

"Go ahead E44."

"Transmit single 10-75," E44 replies, indicating that this is a working full first alarm fire on arrival.

"For the box we have a fire out of two windows on the third floor of a four-story tenement house."

"Manhattan to E44, you have a full first alarm responding, three engines and two trucks."

"E 44, 10-4."

E44 drops three men off in front of the fire building. They immediately go into the classic backstretch: one member mounts the rear step of his engine, places his arm through three folds of hose, gives a strong pull, steps down and drags the hose toward the direction of the fire. The second man grabs another three folds and steps directly to the rear of the engine. The third man grabs another three folds and drags them slightly away from the middle man. All men are now in position. The first man carries his hose with the nozzle to the point of operation in the burning building. The second and third men play out their hose as needed. This is a basic simple operation, but if there are reports of people trapped or hanging out of windows, this operation will take on a different complexion. Self-control is paramount in such severe circumstances and these men must be like horses, racing with blinders on in order to get that line to its only position, the interior hall.

The motor pump operator (MPO) mounts the fire engine and slowly moves towards the nearby hydrant, playing out hose from the rear. He connects to the hydrant and now has his water to supply the hose operations.

Lieutenant Winters of E44 is the first to enter the fire building to find the exact location to direct his men. When they arrive and the uncharged hose is positioned by the fire door of the apartment, he contacts his engine company chauffeur. "E44 to E44 chauffeur."

"E44K."

"Start water in the line."

While water is surging through the hose line I arrive with my Forcible Entry Team of probie Stajk, who carries a six foot hook and fire extinguisher, and Bill Hardy, my senior man carrying an axe and a claw tool which can force open locked doors. Just before E44's water arrives, Stajk empties his two and a half gallon fire extinguisher into the front room fire, holding our tenuous position until the hose line is ready to operate.

I now get the message I've been waiting for.

"Ladder 13 roof to L13."

"L13K."

"Cap, the roof is open and I'm going to the rear fire escape to check conditions."

"10-4," I reply.

The hall is now clearing of smoke and heat and we operate with better visibility.

E44 takes its line, now charged with water, into the front room fire. They point their hose line to the ceiling, producing a rush of steam that smothers the fire. Now they direct it to the fire itself to cool it below its flash point. The fire is out.

I'm just ready to make an examination of the fire location when Lieutenant Winters' and my own handi-talkies blurt out an excitable message from my outside vent, John Thomasion: "L13 O. V. to L13, I have an urgent message!"

All units on the scene immediately stop using their handi-talkies.

"L13 to L13 O. V., go ahead," I say.

"Cap! I'm on the third floor fire escape with Jimmy. He fell, he's bleeding, he's got blood all over his face! Shit! We need an ambulance! Jimmy, don't worry, buddy."

Having fallen through rusty stairs of the fourth floor fire escape, Jimmy lays there bleeding badly from his face, his one leg contorted beneath him. John remains crouched beside him urging him not to move. The occupants of the apartment behind the fire escape had heard his fall and outcry, and hand John towels through their window to staunch Jimmy's bleeding.

"L13 to L13 O. V., we're on the way to the third floor balcony. Is that the correct location?"

"Yeah Cap, hurry, he's bleeding bad!"

The old couple's apartment leading to the fire escape is directly to the rear, from where we are operating. We try the door; it's unlocked, and an old man quickly ushers us through the apartment to the fire escape. Reaching the window, we see John, our O. V. man, holding bloody towels to Jim's face. I get a report from Battalion 10:

"Battalion 10 to L13, ambulance has been called, they're on their way."

In the meantime, knowing that the fire escape may be unstable, I cautiously climb out the window. John shows me a beefy gash that stretches from the right side of Jimmy's forehead, across his eye and down to the corner of his mouth. Jimmy looks like he's going to pass out.

"Cap, I think he's going into shock."

"Somebody get me some blankets!" I yell to the men behind me.

Within seconds, the old man's wife has ripped the blankets from their bed and is handing them to my men with tears in her eyes. John and I cover Jimmy's shoulders to maintain his body heat.

"Stay with us, Jim, don't move. The ambulance is on its way. You're gonna be fine," I say.

"Yeah Jim, fine, but not pretty," says John, trying to add some levity.

Jimmy forces a little smile. "Damn prettier than you." he replies.

The ambulance arrives and soon we meet the paramedics at the window. John and I climb back into the apartment to give them room to work. With rapid precision, the two paramedics — a big hefty guy and a very petite girl who looks thirteen — cut off Jimmy's coat and gently place a cervical brace around his neck. They cut off his pants and we see bone jutting out, his leg bent unnaturally at the knee. Because of the precarious position of the fire escape, the team will splint Jim's leg inside the apartment. With help from John, now back on the fire escape, Jimmy is gently transferred to a gurney on the count of three, his neck and leg carefully stabilized. Jimmy winces and we all respond with words of encouragement. After strapping him up, Jimmy is passed to us through the window.

Safely inside, the paramedics work in unison. One places a blood pressure cuff, oxygen mask, and various other monitors while the other inserts an IV into Jimmy's arm. He is alert and responding to their questions. Good sign.

Later on, Chief McCartney comes out onto the fire escape and we examine the stairs leading from the fourth floor balcony. Three steps are broken through and there are extensive signs of rust. We can easily break off parts of the stairs with our hands.

"Cap, see that all this is documented and followed up with a company inspection. The fire marshals are on the way, should be here any minute," the Chief tells me.

"It's our district, Chief. I'm gonna make sure this is followed through."

We head downstairs and get to the street just as the ambulance is about to pull away.

"John, go with Jimmy to the hospital. After we're done here we'll pick you up."

The Chief, satisfied that the operation is complete, is about to take up and return to quarters.

"Cap, tell the men good job! Wait for the fire marshals. L16 will finish up with the exam of the fire area. You go to the hospital when you're done here, go out of service until you get back to quarters, take some time."

In a few minutes I hear a woman in the crowd, screaming at the top of her lungs, "They're burning us out! These low lifes keep forcing us out of our apartments and they've gone too far this time! That poor fireman. I hope the bastards who did this rot in hell!"

The fire marshals arrive and we return to the fire apartment where I give them their required information about the fire.

"We've had a few fires on this block. The tenants believe its harassment to get them to move and I believe they're right on," I say.

I'm trying to control the hot rage building up in my gut and make a silent promise not to let this incident fall through the cracks.

"Alrighty Cap, we'll finish up here with the scene arson exam and we'll also interview some of the tenants. Jeez, who can blame them for being pissed off."

I'm glad to see fire marshals at the scene again, after their force was so depleted by the city's fiscal restraints.

As we're leaving to go to Metropolitan Hospital on 102nd Street, I talk with some of the bystanders and hear that most of the old supers have been replaced with new nasty ones who are harassing them to make them move out.

"They're very slow in making repairs or giving us heat or hot water. How do they get away with it?" they exclaim.

I tell them, "If there's anything in my power to see who's responsible, I will. I'm going to start with the building owners."

We head to the hospital. John greets us in the waiting area. He asks a nurse, "Please get the doctor who treated Jimmy, if he's available. The Captain's here and he's anxious to know about his condition."

The nurse hurries off and returns with a confident looking young man in scrubs. The amicable young man introduces himself. "I'm the Chief ER Resident. His leg is broken in a few places, Captain. He was in a lot of pain, of course, until we sedated him to set the leg. We're waiting for Plastics to see him. He has extensive laceration to his face. Fortunately it's superficial, no broken bones. The CT scan shows no trauma to his brain."

We're listening intently, hanging on every word. The doctor senses our concern. "Before he went off, he said the only thing he could use right now was a gin and tonic." The doctor laughs, releasing the tension. We all break up. It seems we've been holding our breaths.

"That's Jimmy. He lives in Yorkville. He's always in one bar or another, always laughing and cracking jokes." I say.

We get back to quarters at four a.m., after taking an hour off to change and rest. I lay down for a catnap but can't relax as the anger rumbles inside me.

\* \* \*

Arson is an insidious crime, with its injuries, loss of all earthly possessions of its victims and, too often, deaths. In my nine years in Brooklyn I was often exposed to a type of arson typical in rundown areas and how it works. To induce buying of buildings in ghetto areas, the City gave a three year tax moratorium to new owners, hoping that it would lead to saving property values and neighborhoods. Unfortunately it also opened doors for crooks and arsonists. The new owners gave no services to their tenants for the three years, collected as many rents as possible, got into the assigned risk pool for fire insurance, and then paid some junky a few bucks to burn those buildings down. With very few deterrents or prosecutions, the arsonists had the field all to themselves. This was in addition to "Jewish Lightning," insurance money received by failing businesses for burned-out buildings, the vendetta of fire for revenge and for drug operations that had gone bad. All these types of arson brought misery to the affected innocent pawns.

One such fire in Bushwick had involved tossing a five gallon can of gas on the interior stairs of a wood frame building. The resultant fire was so intense that it burned and completely collapsed the interior stairs through the building. By the time units had arrived, they had to "ladder the stairs" which meant replacing the burned out stairs with ladders from the fire truck so the hose line could reach the next landings. Other hose lines were taken up outside ladders to get to the top floor. There a mother and four children were found dead, their dying fingernail scratches etched into the linoleum floor. It was later determined to be a drug operation that went wrong. This was the poorer end of arson in the ghettos. The rich end was in the desirable real estate areas of Manhattan where the big money was. Known in these circles as "construction vacates," they expedited the removal of old buildings to make room for luxurious hi-rise residential buildings.

In 1978, newly elected Mayor Ed Koch provided hope that he would address this arson issue. The atmosphere was ripe for change and one of his campaign promises was to build the manpower pools of the needed Fire Marshals. He promised a 350 man force to implement the strong laws that were already on the books but almost never prosecuted. He warned building owners that the party was over. If caught, they would go to jail, and he meant it.

# Chapter 2

# AN ARSON CONNECTION

"CAP, YOU WEREN'T in the kitchen for your usual morning coffee so I decided to give you our best hotel service," says Gerry Guilfoyle, bearing two cups of coffee into our bunk room. "Heard about Jimmy getting hurt last night and the rough night you had."

I was surprised to learn I'd slept through the noisy early morning.

"Those dirty sons of bitches get away with murder!" Gerry exclaims.

I take a grateful sip of my coffee, clearing my head. "Gerry, I'd like you to go through our building records for this fire building, update the info on the card and see if anything was reported on the rear fire escape. Go out there and make a physical inspection of the fire building and that rear fire escape. The Marshals responded last night and gave it a Code One high priority because of Jimmy, so their written report should be arriving soon. Keep the battalion informed of all your findings."

"OK, Cap, and I'll let you know too."

A few more sips of coffee cleared my head enough for me to remember that today is the fire house's big semi-final softball game for the City Championship. I had to get a move on. "I want to see Jimmy at the hospital and meet the team in Central Park at 10:30 for the game. After, I'll come back to the firehouse — I'm working a mutual for Lieutenant Floyd who needed the night off — I'll be able to look over your inspection results then."

I shower and dress quickly, grab a roll and more coffee. As I leave for the hospital the firehouse is buzzing, getting ready for the game. I put a note on our bulletin board saying I'd find out when Jimmy can have visitors.

At the hospital I ask for the doctor who treated Jimmy. He arrives after a while and tells me Jimmy is doing much better but is well sedated. "You can say a fast hello, but not much else."

Jimmy looks like he's sleeping but he must have sensed a presence. Slowly, he opens his eyes.

"Hi Jim. How ya doing? On my way to the big game, thought I'd stop by and see you."

"Feeling better Cap. But boy, wish I was goin to the game." he answers drowsily. "Still a big Notre Dame fan," he jokes. "Cap, tell the boys to win one for the Gipper."

"I will, Jimmy. Soon as the game's over we'll call the hospital with the scores."

"That'd be great," he says as he falls back into sleep. I get to the game just in time and see that the grills, the soda and beer are all set up. The guys have completed practice and are ready for the game. I see Eddy Duignan, manager of our softball team, giving some last-minute encouragement to our team. I'm one of the coaches and am also hoping for success. They look a little tense, but that's to be expected. Each of New York's boroughs has a league and today's game is the semi-final playoff for the City Championship.

There are more than 100 softball teams throughout the boroughs and the quality of play is very high. In a field in Central Park, E22 and L13, winners of the Manhattan North and Bronx playoff, are playing the winners of the Manhattan South Staten Island Playoff, L9 and E33 from Great John Street in lower Manhattan. The winner of today's best of three series will play the winner of the Brooklyn-Queens Semi-final for the city championship.

All the men are excited. Ours is a young house, looking to distinguish itself. Working in the shadow of the well-deserved reputations of the ghetto companies in the Bronx and Upper Manhattan, E22 and L13 want to establish their own identity.

E22 and L13 take the first game five to one, E33 and L9 takes the second seven to five. Just before the third game, two black youths suddenly run across the infield, pursued by a policeman who is gradually being outdistanced. He shouts to us, "They stole a woman's purse!" Our team gets the picture and, like a posse from the Old West, take off after the boys. Led by marathon runner, Brendan Sheehan, they quickly catch up and Brendan says to the perps, "Hey, I can run like this all day!" One of the boys responds with bad-mouth invectives and Brendan lands a perfect right cross, knocking him down. The other firemen corral his accomplice and the two punks are administered a little street justice. The huffing patrolman arrives before serious damage is done and arrests them.

We return to the field for some beers and food before starting the third game. It goes to the bottom of the final seventh inning. Bill Regan, our center fielder and an outstanding athlete, hits a home run with two outs and the bases loaded. We win!

I eat some more of the wonderful food and slug down a few beers with our team, then return to our quarters around 2:00 p.m. for some sleep. The rest of the men who won't be working the night shift go to Carlow's East, our favorite watering hole on Lexington between 84th and 85th streets. We love to hang out at Carlow's. Not only is it just two long-wood golf shots from our firehouse, but it's populated by a blue-collar crowd, with a few notables who love the company of this crowd.

In quarters, I call the hospital and leave a message for Jimmy about today's win. I also leave the firehouse number and ask them to let us know when it will be okay for Jimmy to have visitors. Dog-tired from the night before, I lay down in the bunk area of our office and fall into a deep sleep.

Later, Gerry enters our office. The clock reads five o'clock. He waits until I shake off my grogginess and fills me in on the results of his investigation.

"Cap, Wainwright Management's the new owner of the buildings, the fire building and the four others connected to it. Looks like they were bought up about two years ago just after our last inspection. I already updated the building cards with new ownership and building info."

"How's the fire escape?" I ask, putting on my socks and shoes.

"Not in good shape. A lot of loose and rusty stairs — a disaster waitin' to happen. I issued a Forthwith."

In addition to the Forthwith which is a violation order for immediate compliance, Gerry tells me he'll post warnings on the hazardous condition of the fire escape tomorrow. Digesting this, I can see Gerry's aggravated. "Yeah, what else Gerry?" I ask.

"I also got a lot of feedback from the occupants of the buildings since Wainwright came on board. All their complaints were like the ones we heard about from Emily. Cap, how can these bastards get away with this blatant harassment? It's not right, not to mention criminal. I'd love to get my hands on them."

It's not hard to imagine what that would be like, looking at Gerry's huge hands and arms which always reminded me of big Stillson wrenches. Gerry was talking about an elderly tenant, Emily Bauman, who lived across from the firehouse and always visited us with cakes and cookies in exchange for a cup of coffee and conversation. One day she came to quarters very upset about what the new owners were doing. The owners had replaced the old super with one of their supers. Water leaks, no hot water and other inconveniences were happening too often to be legit. I remembered one incident well. One morning a few men and I were standing in the front of quarters, as usual admiring the bevy of business girls who strode past the firehouse on their way to work. We loved the everyday parade of good-looking women who always smiled back at us, many flirtatiously. Suddenly Emily crossed the street, looking distressed.

"*Kaptan*!" she exclaimed in her thick German accent, "Dat mean super is in our building again — can not you do zometing?"

I looked over and saw Gerry's jaw tighten. "Cap, let's go talk to this creepy bastard."

I knew Gerry was capable of anything at that moment. We could see the creep standing across the street in front of Emily's building. I shot Gerry a look that said 'calm down' and we walked over to this guy. The super saw us coming; didn't even have to open his mouth for me to already know he was one obsequious snake. Probably suspecting a confrontation, the super smiled to us and extended his hand. We did not respond. Gerry moved menacingly close to the super.

"Look, you fucking slime ball, we know what you're up to and if anything else happens — and you know exactly what I'm talkin' about — you're going to have to deal with us. You got it, pal?"

So much for calming Gerry down, but now I find I'm ready for confrontation with this skell as well. "We've been watching this operation for a while," I tell him.

The super's nervous now. He knows better than to butt heads with me or Gerry. I explain to him that the Fire Marshal Enforcement Unit has been notified and that his activities are being recorded. In my periphery, I can see Gerry looking surprised because, of course, I'd just made this up, but I'm on a roll now. "Koch has beefed up our arson enforcement and promised if we catch you, all you sons a bitches are going to jail." As we turn and walk away, I tell him, "If you're smart as you think you are, you'll heed this little advice."

Sure enough, two days later we hear from Emily that he's quit and they're looking for the old super to hire him back.

I remember how good that incident made us feel. One for the good guys.

I'm brought back to the present by Gerry, who says, "I'm goin up to Carlow's to celebrate our win before I drive home to New Jersey." I nod.

"I'm in to relieve you tomorrow morning, Cap — and who knows, if I get lucky tonight, I just might sleep at the firehouse." He saunters out with a chuckle.

At 6:00 p.m. we call the roll of incoming men reporting to

duty for both companies and give them their assignments as well as the news about Jimmy. I go to the kitchen for a cup of coffee. My chauffeur, Joe Moore, tells me we have to go out and purchase the evening meal; this month is L13's turn. We assemble all members, advising the dispatcher that we are going to purchase the evening meal and are ready for all responses via radio. It's off to Gristedes Supermarket on Lexington. While the men are grocery shopping, Joe and I discuss today's softball game. He is a senior man and one of our team coaches. Joe, a laconic wry type, doesn't usually say much, but he talks about today's win with a rare animation. The firemen return with the groceries and its back to quarters. I ask what's for supper and they say, "Spaghetti with sausages and meatballs and toasted garlic bread."

My favorite!

"Also ice cream and strawberries to follow."

Does it get any better than this?

After the groceries are stashed we're told that we'll eat dinner about nine o'clock, after the nightly training drill. After the drill and critique of the unconfirmed arson fire on the previous night, the importance of the first line to protect the interior stairways is stressed, and we are also reminded how important it is that the roof be opened to relieve smoke, heat and gases. These are probably the two most important parts of operations. All other things such as searches, forcible entry, venting — all equally important — are made easier if those initial operations take place.

At 8:30 p.m. I return to my office to see how Victor is doing. He looks content and sluggish, his belly full and working. I look at his I.D. card on the tank and can't help but smile. I decide to call the police precinct to find out the results of this afternoon's incident and if any witnesses are needed. To my chagrin, I'm told that the woman whose purse was snatched will not press charges. Probably afraid. The "perps" were let go. The only satisfaction from this incident was the punishment exacted in the park by our team.

The house watchman informs me on the intercom that I have a visitor, a woman with a complaint. As I approach the house watch desk, she introduces herself as Yolanda Echevaria. "I live on 91st Street between York and East End," this attractive dark haired woman tells me. She is small but athletic looking with confident body language. She tells me there was a fire at her apartment and she'd like to tell me about the circumstances involved. I invite her into my office and place a chair for her. She sees the ashtray on my desk and asks if it is okay to light up.

"Of course," I reply and light her cigarette and my own. I introduce myself and ask, "What's the problem?"

"I believe the fire in my apartment was arson. I'm a writer, working on a book about my life story. A publishing company gave me a big advance and a ghostwriter to help me. This has something to do with the arson. My book is about my experience as a CIA agent who was once sent to Cuba to murder Fidel Castro. I now think that certain aspects of my book involve people still in public life or office and they're trying to intimidate me into not writing it. I think the fire at my apartment is a warning."

"Was the fire reported to be suspicious?" I ask.

"Don't know, I wasn't home. I was at my house in Ossining. With the advance book money, I rented a home in Westchester County for me and my two children so they could attend private school. "

"When did it happen? "

"A week ago today. My apartment's super is a good friend. He's moved me into a temporarily available apartment next door until my place is livable again."

"Normally a Fire Report takes six to eight weeks for public access. I'll check the Battalion's Report for any particulars available."

Her apartment is on my way home. Intrigued, I offer to drop by in the morning to look at the scene and discuss any particulars in the Fire Report. "I'll be home, and I'm glad something is happening. "

I escort her to the front of the firehouse, where she gets into a beautiful silver 1978 Lincoln. She waves and is off.

Ten minutes later, the intercom announces that dinner is on the table. A Battalion Chief and his driver, two companies, E22 and L13, six men each, for a total of 14, sit at the table. Spaghetti, sausages and meatballs, would definitely be a consideration for a last meal request. Hopefully, no alarms. About one in four meals are interrupted by what we're paid to do. Snatch a meatball and go; be careful that all stoves are off. At least two firehouses have returned to put out fires in their own kitchens.

We're in luck and get to eat uninterrupted. Sitting around the large kitchen table afterward, most of us light up and the usual firehouse banter begins. Jobs, politics, sports, cooking. Always animated, controversial with an array of different opinions, especially on sports and politics. Cooler heads prevail if it gets too personal and could lead to some hard feelings but, like in a family, it is always resolved. Eating, living and sleeping together, the firehouse is like a second home for all of us, which breeds a close familiarity. At moments like this — full bellies after an uninterrupted meal — we know how lucky we are and how we love our jobs. Eventually, Hagar (a.k.a. Gus Peterson), gently reminds the probies of their position in this hierarchy and that it's time to go to work. Dishes, pots and pans are collected, table cleared, floors swept; they do it with an enthusiasm that shows they aren't unhappy with this position. The observing senior men who have great interest, knowledge, and preparation for their job, are the catalysts that shapes their discipline and the teamwork needed for our job. Officers, some good, some bad, come and go, but the senior men, the informal leaders, are the ones that hold the continuity of our job. They are the mortar that keeps it all together; they are the infantry of the fire service.

# Chapter 3

# YOLANDA

I'M IN THE kitchen at 7:30 the next morning having coffee and a cigarette. Gerry Guilfoyle, my incoming relief for the 9 to 6 day tour, arrives early as usual and has coffee with me. We exchange company information and occurrences that have come up since we last saw each other: personnel problems, things needed for the ladder truck or firehouse, any upcoming events, etc. It's always on my second tour ending and his first that we see each other. Once that's out of the way, I ask about his family, kids and the like. With Jerry being divorced and me separated, we both have to arrange time with our children.

We had gone on vacation together one summer, in the upstate Adirondack Mountains near Canada, where Jerry had rented a campsite with a small trailer. We'd taken my youngest daughter Mary and his two daughters— all between the ages of ten and thirteen. All of us have unforgettable memories of the beautiful

Adirondacks, the seaplane ride over the huge lakes, the barbeques, sleeping in his trailer, even the bear breaking into our garbage. He and I had gotten very close on that trip. I tell him I'm going to stop off to see this woman who came into quarters last night with an improbable story. He's at once curious and interested. After a shower, I go down to the office for a nother cup of coffee with Jerry, discuss Victor's last feeding, then leave.

It's a beautiful morning so I decide to walk the ten blocks and not have to worry about parking on the crowded streets. I know a good luncheonette for breakfast at York and 91st, halfway down the block from where Lou Gehrig grew up. There was once a plaque on the building, You can still see the discolored image of it. Just as well its gone. The way the neighborhood is changing, it would probably get stolen today. I can still see Gehrig's mother in the movie, "The Pride of the Yankees," looking out the kitchen window of their tenement onto a dirt ball field calling her son home for dinner.

After a hearty breakfast, I walk the half block from the luncheonette to Yolanda's building. She answers with a smile and a cigarette in hand. We sit and chat over coffee and cigarettes. I ask if I can look at the burned out next door apartment; yes, she knows the super. We enter the tiny three room apartment. I sniff around for an accelerant, then look for any alligatoring which can signify the starting point of a fire. Nothing seems unusual. I note that she, a heavy smoker, had left her apartment the morning of the fire to go to her Westchester house. A cigarette smoldering in a couch or bed can take hours to ignite. The fire was reported at 1:00 a.m. Since there was no means of contacting her, she only learned of the fire when she returned three days later.

We return to her temporary apartment and I inform her that the chief's report showed no indication of arson and "I'll get an official confirmation of your visit to our quarters and notify the chief of your fears."

Then we talk about her life.

"I received $350,000 for the book I'm to write about my life story. With that money I rented the house in Ossining and bought two horses for my kids. I have a live-in nanny who cares for them when I'm in the city."

"What about your early life?" I ask.

"My father was the Spanish captain of a tanker ship, The Madrid. It regularly stopped at Cuba and during summer school breaks I'd take trips with him. When I was sixteen, I met Fidel Castro in Havana. He liked me and we become friends. A few years later it developed into a relationship. About that time Dad was getting nervous over the situation in Cuba; he took me home and forbade me to return.

"The CIA found out about my relationship with Castro. They contacted me and wanted to know more. When I was twenty-one I moved to the U.S. and became a citizen. I looked back on my Castro tryst as a short innocuous affair; didn't think much of it. But the CIA made me an offer: they wanted me to become an agent and work for them. They were after Castro and looking for opportunities to get near him. So I became an agent, acting as part of a covert operation."

She showed me a picture of her in Marco Island, Florida, along with one of the bigwigs of the agency. A plot was hatched, involving her going to Cuba to rekindle her affair with Castro. Several trips later the CIA concocted a plan to kill him with poison pellets hidden in a cold cream jar.

"On my mission, I found out I couldn't do it. Besides, the pellets melted in the cold cream jar."

This sounded unbelievable, but she showed me pictures and an accompanying newspaper story describing the unsuccessful plot. I swallowed that and changed the subject.

"I'm interested in writing myself. Just how does a person go about getting a book published?" I told her about a story I'd written that was published in *The Fire House*, a trade magazine. It was a short story about our firehouse being held hostage when the city planned to close several firehouses. "They looked at maps of the city and, if two fire houses were in close proximity, one would be closed," I explained. "My Engine Company, E218, was slated to be closed in spite of the very heavy loss of life in the Bushwick neighborhood of wood frame buildings. It was considered one of the highest red zones in the city, known as The Triangle of Death based on the number of lives lost there."

"I'd like to read the article," Yolanda said. "I'll mention it to the publisher's ghostwriter. I have an appointment with him next week."

I make a date to visit when she will be getting interviewed, then invite her out for lunch. She happily agrees and off we go.

As we're finishing lunch, she asks, "Could you do me a favor and help me and my girlfriend move a few pieces of heavy furniture at her apartment on 80th Street?"

I agree and we take her new Lincoln which she has treated herself to with some of the advanced money. It's a beautiful silver car.

We park in the underground garage of a big hi-rise residential building and take the elevator to the 20th floor. Monique greets us at her door, all excited, and thanks me for being so nice. She is very easy on the eyes, with flowing wavy red hair and a great body. I'm impressed with the striking colors and attractive look of her apartment. Even an unknowing eye like mine could tell she'd given a lot of care and attention to her home. After moving the few pieces, which didn't amount to much, we sit for coffee and I find Monique outgoing and easy to talk with.

Much later, Yolanda and I depart and she confides that Monique is a high end "Escort Gal" making a very good living. My only thought was that her dates must be well satisfied. Yolanda offers to drop me off at the firehouse, and on the way she chats about how Monique decorated her apartment. "It looks like it was professionally done, but she did it all by herself. She has very good taste. You can't imagine how expensive the furniture was that we helped her move."

I'm thinking it's quite a spread of interests between her working job and her other creative talents. Yes, a very interesting person!

# Chapter 4

# ARSON AND CIVIL DISOBEDIENCE

I WAS ON MY three days off after a two-night tour when I heard the disturbing news that a captain and two firemen had been badly injured at a fire on 105th Street between 2nd and Lexington. While entering the smoke-filled hallway of a vacant four-story tenement where a basement fire had been reported, two firemen and a captain had fallen through the floor to the basement.

Arson once again had raised its ugly head, this time as one of the tools of civil disobedience by groups such as the Black Liberation Army, black Muslim splinter groups and any other group with a bitch against the system.

Someone had intentionally covered over a hole in the first floor hallway with a 4x8 foot piece of plywood, placed so that anyone standing on it would fall through. Even though the building was reported vacant, we are obligated to treat it as occupied until proven otherwise. Squatters could have been living there. One rule, always the same, is to protect the hallway. The perps knew this and had deliberately set the basement fires under these hallways, aware that their evil crime would hurt or kill firemen. The trails of volatile accelerants discovered later in the basement proved that this was an act of arson.

In that smoky first floor hallway, the captain and firemen had stepped on the loose plywood and fallen directly into the cellar fire. A third fireman who just missed falling in heard their yells and, using superhuman strength, grabbed the captain while the fireman below pushed him up. Once out, he and the firemen pulled the remaining man from the burning basement.

The captain, whom I knew very well, suffered the effects of a super-heated body — something victims seldom survive. The firefighter who had pushed the captain up had severely burned and blackened hands along with the super-heating. The other firefighter's burns weren't as serious since he hadn't fallen into the fire. They were immediately transferred to the Fire Department Burn Center Unit at New York Hospital. The captain was placed in ICU with serious burns over much of his body. The fireman had burned his hands so badly that he lost most of his fingers.

While on my day tour a few days later, I took our tower ladder with the working team to the Burn Center to visit them. I'd called ahead to make sure they could receive visitors. The lesser-burned fireman had been treated and released on the second day. The captain was in a tent for infection prevention and could not be seen. The other fireman had big white bandages on both hands. Neither of them would ever return to full duty and were given the choice of staying on light duty as long as they liked or of retiring on disability.

As we left the hospital I felt a white hot anger I could barely control. I thought of the perpetrators and their obvious intent to kill firemen, men who had gone there to help. For what reason? Hatred for the establishment, for authority? What possessed their evil minds?

I thought of the Burn Center Unit too, and the superior care the firemen were getting. Ten years ago the Burn Center Unit in New York Hospital consisted of a mere one or two beds. In all of New York there was only one other small unit, in Columbia Presbyterian Hospital. In a city the size of New York, these paltry facilities could never have handled a major catastrophe. In an event with extensive numbers of victims, burn patients would have needed to be transferred to other cities' burn facilities.

Fortunately, ten years ago four firemen decided that the lack of these special units was intolerable. The men created an organization called The Fire Department Burn Center, which raised money to support a burn center big enough to help handle the needs of the city. Beautiful red velvet memorial cards were sold. Many golf outings, dances, benefits and even musicals were arranged to increase donations for beds and equipment. Lt. James Curran, among other firefighters, was committed to fundraising for the burn units. Thanks to them and the big corporations which responded very generously, there were now fourteen beds and state-of-the-art equipment to handle burn victims.

I thought again about the men we had just visited in the enhanced burn center and decided to be grateful for this improvement. We weren't ending arson-set fires, but at least we were now able to take care of the firemen who suffered from them.

I was reminded of my first exposure to this type of hatred by a black Muslim group on Bushwick Avenue in Brooklyn.

Bushwick had been the hub of the elite and rich in its heyday at the turn of the 20th century. The street was mostly lined with large Queen Ann houses with wraparound porches and other mansion-type homes. On one of the Queen Annes a plaque bore the quote, "Dr. Livingston I presume?" This had been the house of Dr. David Livingston, an anti-slavery advocate and three-time explorer of the Africa continent who had given Victoria Falls its name. Livingston had gone missing on one of his explorations. When he was found by Henry Morgan Stanley in a small African village, Morgan had famously said, "Dr. Livingston, I presume?"

On a regular building inspection, one of the Bushwick Avenue buildings slated to be inspected was a Community Center. It was painted red with a black wrought iron fence enclosing an immaculate green lawn — the red, black and green of the black power symbol. Walking up on the newly paved walkway, I was met at the door on the huge wrap-around porch by two men in business suits who looked like they belonged on Wall Street.

"I'm on a routine inspection and we'll be inspecting the entire premises for the next two hours or so," I informed them.

With expressionless steely faces, they told me that the building was run by the Black Liberation Movement and that we had no jurisdiction there.

"Are you refusing us entry? I asked.

Not surprisingly, they answered, "yes."

Avoiding a confrontation, I withdrew to the sidewalk and called the 35th Battalion Chief to the scene. When he arrived I explained the circumstances and he wisely said he would contact Department Headquarters for a course of action. He told me to inspect another building in the meantime.

About two hours later, the chief met us at the building we

were inspecting and informed me I was not to inspect the Center but to return to quarters. In quarters he told me that the Department had been told by the F.B.I that the group was under their surveillance and that the Fire Department was to back off. "Gene, they probably have infiltrated this group with undercover agents and want things status quo."

About a month later we received a report of smoke coming from the Center. We pulled up and I ordered a line stretched to the front gate. Telling my men to stand fast, I entered the yard and was met by the same two militants as before — probably guards — who informed me that they were in charge and the fire was under control. With that, many people started running out in a panic, with red watery eyes and handkerchiefs held to their faces.

"Hey pal, do you want us to put out the fire or what?" I asked point-blank, fed up with their horseshit.

Their now panicky response was, "Yes!"

It was a kitchen grease fire which was made worse by their attempts to put it out themselves. We stretched the line to the kitchen area and easily put it out. Meanwhile, the other units had arrived and made their usual examination of all parts of the building. Trying not to show our satisfaction, we took our line out the front door. I looked at the somewhat soured congregation and did not throw fuel on another fire.

I understood them. Blacks had suffered lack of employment, poor housing, unfair treatment and prejudice. I realized that the searing zeal of their youth and the many injustices Blacks had suffered had brought about this level of hatred and violent actions. In the same situation, I might well have reacted the same. However, two wrongs don't make a right. These incidents showed that their civil disobedience made them no better than their persecutors who abused and denied them.

Two months after this incident there was a shootout at John-Al's Sporting Goods Store on Broadway near Myrtle. A Black Muslim Militant group was robbing the store with the intent to steal as many guns, ammo and rifles as they could. An employee slipped out a side door and called the police. While the unknowing perps were getting set to load up a van parked outside, the cops had arrived and a shootout erupted from within the store. One cop was killed and lay in the street while another was wounded and sought refuge behind an elevated train pillar. A standoff ensued with police S.W.A.T. teams soon arriving.

Our engine company was called to stand by at the scene in case the police used smoke bombs or tear gas, which is highly incendiary to a wood frame building such as this. Parked on Myrtle just short of Broadway, we hooked up to a hydrant and stretched a precautionary line to the nearest safe point of operation. Hearing a metallic rumble, we peered cautiously around the corner and saw, coming down Broadway, a large Army armored personnel carrier moving our way. It stopped between the dead policeman and the store and removed him into their carrier. They then moved near the "El" pillar to pick up the wounded cop.

Meanwhile the owner-hostage somehow escaped through an exit the robbers didn't know existed. He led the S.W.A.T. team back into the store and they caught the robbers completely by surprise. Faced with this array of firepower, they surrendered without a struggle*. It was later learned that this group was connected to the building on Bushwick Avenue. They were probably looking to make it an armed camp.

---

*See newspaper article on page 189.

# Chapter 5

# THE FBI

AFTER OUR GUT-wrenching win in last week's semi-final, this week's softball game is for the Championship of New York City. With over 100 teams involved, it's a gigantic occasion for the whole Fire Department. I am to work the day tour on Wednesday and Thursday and the game will be on Friday in Central Park, again the best of three games.

On Wednesday everybody is excited about the big game. We have a meeting and decide, win or lose, we're going to throw a party at Carlows East after the game and invite everybody. The game will be well attended so there'll be a lot of preparation. A house tax assessment of $50.00 for each man will cover the drinks and food, which will be prepared Thursday at the firehouse and transported to Carlows. We'll make trays of baked sausages and peppers, ziti with sliced meatballs, baked chicken in mushroom sauce as well as macaroni, potato and coleslaw salads.

A roast beef will be cooked and sliced for sandwiches; cheese, hors d'oeuvres and salty snacks will also be provided. Not a small operation. In addition to Carlow's patrons we could easily draw over 100 people. With 60 men in our firehouse's two companies we'll have at least $3,000 to make a splash to be remembered by our fire department brothers.

On Wednesday I get an unusual call from an FBI agent, Bill Wilson. He wants to interview me regarding a case they're investigating. Tomorrow, a female agent, Elizabeth Peters, will visit me at 11:00 a.m., he tells me. He doesn't give me any particulars, saying that she'll explain everything. He adds, as an afterthought, that Elizabeth is an ex-nun who became a FBI agent after leaving her order. With this and the preparations for Friday's game, tomorrow should be an interesting day.

After work today we'll all head over to Carlows to prepare for Friday. Jim Hyland and Billy Byrnes, the two owners, are almost as excited as our firemen about the occasion. Every year Carlows East patrons and our firehouse hold a softball game in Central Park, for the bragging rights in the neighborhood. Food at the game is always prepared and supplied by our firehouse. The beer, soda and drinks for both the game and after-game celebration are paid for by Billy and Jim. We're good at this!

We have a wonderful evening meal at Carlows. Pizza is delivered from two doors away. Tonight I'll stay over at the firehouse which always has ample beds for such occasions.

Thursday morning I get up early, shower, have coffee, relieve Lieutenant Gilfoyle early and start my day. The firehouse is a bundle of energy with off-duty men coming in to lay out the next day's party itinerary. They're experienced at this and, as usual, everything is going well.

At 11:00, the house watchman announces that I had a visitor. I'm not quite prepared for the stunning, tall brunette who enters my office with presence, elegance and class. She shows me her FBI identity card and introduced herself and then spots Victor the Constrictor. She is instantly interested. After she checks Victor's I.D., she and I are totally at ease.

I am surprised to learn that there is a federal investigation of Wainwright Management's method of acquiring the land and buildings where two of their luxury buildings have been built. She asks me for all records of the buildings that formerly stood on these sites. The FBI is interested in 20 such locations. I check my dead record file for demolished buildings. Some had been demolished as a result of fires and some for being vacant. The old building records and related folders had notations of previous suspicious fires that had been investigated, concluding they had been arson. Even with the limited fire investigation available, the picture was perfectly clear. I turned all the records over to Elizabeth, who gave me a receipt. The case against Wainwright Management was ongoing, and she explained that the most positive case they had against them was the RICO act — illegal use of the U.S. mail — which had been created for the war against organized crime.

Over coffee in the kitchen, I learned that Elizabeth came from a New York City Irish civil service family and she was very comfortable being here. Needless to say, all the firemen present went ape over her, and she was enjoying herself as least as much. She mentioned that her dad was a retired New York City policeman and her uncle a fire chief whom I had known. She finished her coffee, said goodby to everyone and left the firehouse.

This day turned out to be interesting and pleasant and I

hoped I'd see the beautiful Elizabeth again. There had been a lot of unusual circumstances arise lately, and they were all pointing me in one direction. Both Yolanda's and Elizabeth's revelations seemed to be prodding me to take action. Was this a call to pursue the evil of arson that bothered me so much?

# Chapter 6

# THE BIG GAME

AFTER MY TWO day tours, I head for Long Beach where I share a house with Dick Keenan, an old friend from E218 days in Brooklyn. After 20 years of marriage, my wife and I had separated two years ago. The marriage hadn't been working. She was willing to stick it out, I wasn't. This decision left me feeling guilty, mainly about the kids, and I tend to block it out with heavy drinking. At the time of the separation my son Gene was 18, Ann 15 and Mary 10. Over the years all my kids have been with me at the firehouse many times while I was working a day tour. At this time Gene Jr. is ready to go into the Navy, After high school, Ann moved in with a girlfriend and has a job in Manhattan. Mary is with her Mother and the one I worry and feel bad about. All the financial aspects have been taken care of. I see all my children often. They love Long Beach and Dick's house which is a stone's throw to the beautiful beach and ocean.

On the way home, I first stop and pick up Mary, who will be staying over with me so she can come to Central Park for tomorrow's big game.

After dropping her overnight bag at the house, Mary and I walk the beach and wait for the sunset. We sit on the long rock jetty on one particular rock which we have named Contemplation Rock. It's a flat rock so big that we can lay on it and almost fall asleep. After a disappointing sunset (too many dark clouds) we head back to Dick's house to change for dinner at Chauncey's, a bar and restaurant right on the beach. Our favorite meal is pork tidbits on garlic bread with melted mozzarella cheese and smothered with duck sauce. Mary always enjoyed Chauncey's, another hangout for cops and firemen. She knows quite a few of the guys from her many visits to Long Beach and to the firehouses where I worked. They always came over to greet her and make a fuss over her.

Mary seems pretty well adjusted to the separation. Things are going well for her at school and she's looking forward to her summer vacation. She's joined the swim team in Levittown where she lives, and is on the Little League girls' softball team. "I even know how to figure out batting averages," she tells me. Mary is articulate and outspoken and sometimes we get into pretty deep conversations. I once asked her if she could give me suggestions about things that could improve the world. One of the her suggestions was, "When the world leaders are meeting, they should each be given a plate of ice cream, because I never saw anyone unhappy and not smiling when they were eating ice cream!" I think she was onto something. I reminded her of this conversation while we were finishing our dinner. She grinned and said, "Let's start with us, Dad, and go for ice cream when we leave Chauncey's!" She's full of good ideas!

Early the next morning Mary and I drive to the firehouse. I have coffee and Mary has a soda while we wait for the ball-players and spectators to leave for Central Park. There's ample parking, which allows us to bring lots of equipment, barbeque grills, food, beer and soda for the games. We set up the field for the 10:30 start, for the best of three games.

As in all sports, to win it has to be your time. Sometimes you seem to get all the breaks. The play that gives us the first game is a tag play at third base. Wally Torres, our catcher, is on second base with a runner on first. Ed Duignan, our designated hitter, belts a line drive between the left and center fielders. Wally scores easily and the runner on first also scores on a close play at home. Suddenly there's a lot of yelling at third base. The third baseman is screaming, "He never touched the bag; it wasn't even close!" They appeal to the umpire. He signals that our guy is safe and pandemonium breaks loose. As first base coach, I ask the third base coach, Joe Moore what he thinks about it. "He wasn't even close," Joe confides, but says nothing — which is what you do in sports. Their third baseman is livid and appeals for fair play. It just isn't done, and the argument pursues. He appeals to me. "It isn't my call," I tell him and he replies, "You have no integrity! You're full of shit!" I react to the insult and we go jaw to jaw, "I want you after the game," he demands and I agree that we'll settle it then. On the sidelines, Mary is sitting on the hood of a car with the daughter of the third baseman who was yelling in my face. The girls look nervous and the expressions they wear says, how could two grown men act like kids. They agree that it is ridiculous though amusing.

The play opens the door for more runs and we win the first game going away. Now to the impending confrontation between me and the third baseman.

We head for the middle of the diamond. With menacing looks, we know what's going to happen. He grabs me and I grab him. "I love you, brother," is the final call. We laugh and then look to our two girls; they look relieved and amused. Between games, both teams join together over hot dogs and beer.

In the second of three games we again seem to get all the breaks and win going away. It gives us the City Championship!

Bedlam breaks loose. The delirium of victory is indescribable. I can now understand why big league ballplayers roll on the ground like little kids after winning a world series. This game to us was just as big. Seeing our guys in a pile, rolling on the ground, is something that will stick in my memory for many years! Eventually we leave the park and head for Carlows. The raucous, happy group arrives and is on a real high. Some of the losing team arrives, and they are our guests. At each important game, they hoist me to the top of the bar and I have to make a victory speech. I am getting used to this and have come up with a theme from Grantland Rice, a famous sports writer: "It isn't whether you win or lose, it's how you play the game," with accolades to the losing team.

Liam, the nine year old son of Billy Byrnes, one of the Carlow owners, is there for "a day" with Dad. Billy introduces me to Liam. After Liam walks away, Billy tells me that he hates girls and will not even talk to them. I tell Mary about Liam, and she walks over to him, grabs his shirt and tells him that she's heard he doesn't like girls. Mary, who can be as intimating as any 12 year old gets, says, "I don't care if you don't like girls, you're going to like me." Liam looks at her, says nothing. As she walks away Liam follows behind her. Mary had somehow hit a button and from then on Liam did whatever she said when they were together, and liked it!

Everyone enjoys the day, eating and drinking from four until 11 o'clock. The owners tell me the only day that compares with this is St. Patrick's Day. (Carlows is at the end of the parade route and is one of the favorite watering holes for the fire department marching contingents). Other companies stop by to wish us well and congratulate us on winning. Men off duty after six o'clock head over and it turns out to be one spectacular party. Truly a great day for our young and trying-harder firehouse.

*The thrill of victory.*

# Chapter 7

# GHOST WRITER

A WEEK AFTER OUR championship win, Yolanda called to tell me when her ghostwriter was coming to interview her. I told her I'd be there and would bring my article. She explained that the interviews usually lasted five to six hours as her various CIA experiences are reviewed.

After sitting through the long and tiring interview with the ghostwriter, we all went through the burned out apartment next door to her backyard for a few beers. Her yard, small but filled with very pretty trees and foliage, was a part of the symphony of similar backyards abutting the backs of buildings on 90th and 91st streets, looking like a unique corridor in a forest.

Her ghostwriter had been involved in many famous books, one of which was about the notorious and flamboyant bank robber, Willie Sutton. While we enjoyed our beers he read my short story and said I should pursue writing; that I seemed to have a natural flair. The whole experience was exciting and full of information for me.

When he left, Yolanda and I decided to go for an early dinner at one of her favorites, a Cuban restaurants on 75th near Third Avenue. We rode there in her silver Lincoln.

She is greeted happily there by the waiters and waitresses and after a few introductions we are seated. She asks me what I like and orders our meals in Spanish. I compliment her on this skill and she tells me she also speaks fluent French and German. My gin martini, the food and the ambiance were the best.

With no rush, we talk. Her career with the CIA lasted about a decade. After leaving the CIA she moved to New York City. Soon she became an auxiliary policeman and became involved with a few members of the New York Police Department. She seemed to love getting into intriguing edgy situations. Many of her CIA and police experiences were going to be in her book. She seemed smart and loaded with information, some of which was spectacular.

She was also very interested in the fire department and easily grasped the things I told her. Somehow the conversation gets around to arson, and after I told her of my visit from the FBI and mentioned the involved Wainwright Management, she said, "I know who is actually setting the fires."

I said nothing, waiting for her to continue.

"Danny O, also known as *La Torcia*," she says, and tells me that after setting the fires, his m.o. is to go to the roof of a tenement across the street from the fire and watch. She also knows the president of Wainwright Management and tells me that her friend Monique lives in one of his buildings, "You remember, where we went to help her move the furniture." Monique's rent is exchanged for her services.

After some prodding she gives me the building president's name, David Maier, and tells me he runs the whole show. "After exhausting the options of no heat or no hot water, or cash payments to move, finally as a last resort he gives the okay to burn them out."

I'm burning this information into my memory, never taking my eyes off of her.

"He has a beautiful penthouse apartment on 76th and Second Avenue," she continues. "In fact I'm invited there for a big birthday bash for him on July 29th." An easy date to remember … it's also my birthday!

# Chapter 8

# NEXT MEETING WITH YOLANDA

ON MY NEXT set of night tours, Yolanda called. She is going to her home in Ossining and asked if I'd like to ride along to see what it's like. She also mentioned that she'd thought of a few things of interest about Wainwright Management. I tell her that day one and two of my three days off are free and I'll come around to her apartment when I leave the firehouse.

When Lieutenant Guilefoyle relieves me after my second night tour I tell him about today's trip to Ossining. He's very interested in what's taking place and starts to kid me with a knowing smile. He gives me a playful jab to my shoulder. I wink, return the jab and say goodbye.

I leave my car at the firehouse and walk over to 91st to meet Yolanda; we'll be taking her car. It's the middle of July and the day is beautiful. As we head upstate, I'm anticipating seeing that wealthy section of New York with the breathtaking scenery and beautiful homes I've heard about. The ride is interesting. Yolanda is intriguing; listening to her is almost like reading a book of adventure stories. She talks abut gun running with the CIA in Marco Island (she promises to show me pictures to back up her story); her disinvolvement with the CIA and then her 10-year involvement with a New York Police Department Inspector, where she discovered the arson connection between Wainwright Management and organized crime.

Since she believes that the fire in her apartment was set to discourage her from going forward with her book, she tells me that she's now getting scared. "There are still people in public office who are connected to my story and the arson job on my place could be a warning."

Since I was on the police department for five years before joining the fire department, I recognized her use of cop jargon in describing some of the incidents in her book.

We stop at an Ossining supermarket for some supplies for the special dinner she wants to cook me. "My kids are away in summer camp, and their nanny has gone to visit her family," she tells me with lowered eyelashes.

Her house is a big ranch house on a huge property. I see two horses grazing in the back. Yolanda puts away the food and makes us ham and cheese sandwiches for lunch. We take our coffee into her living room and she brings out all her albums and scrapbooks and continues to tell me of her escapades, backing them up with pictures and newspaper articles. There is plenty of documentation for what she's talking about, so I know these are not made up stories — not the made-up bullshit they would seem like without these proofs.

Late in the afternoon we stop reading and have a couple of martinis out on her patio. She leaves me outside as she goes in to prepare our dinner. We sit in her very pleasant dinning room for a Cuban meal I had never before tasted, of pork, rice and plenty of veggies mixed in a great sauce. We spend the evening with drinks and more stories about her life.

"Tell me more about fire department operations," she asks. Her questions are good and she seems very interested. Her knowledge of the police auxiliary department where she served for six years and her experience with her ex-boyfriend, a police department inspector, started a lively dialogue between us.

"I know a fire captain who's a double agent with the CIA and has been to Cuba many times through Mexico," she announces.

I ask and she tells me his name and I knew him. He was a lieutenant in Brooklyn and then a captain in upper Manhattan. There was speculation around the job on how he was involved in some type of government operations but they were only rumors.

She told me another story, about a fire in a hi-rise building on 86th and Third Avenue. A big drug operation was linked to the building management.

"The building's super dug up a lot of the harassment supers that replaced legitimate supers — you know, to make the old tenants move. This super was the one who contacted Danny O when his services were needed."

"I remember this one. The fire department responded to a pretty serious fire and accessed sensitive parts of the building while putting it out."

"Yeah. Someone walked out of the building loaded with U.S. currency from drug operations and it was suspected that a fire-man did it."

"This happened about five years ago, right?

"Yes, about then."

I made a note to myself to make some subtle inquiries about sudden retirements, transfers, lotto winners and so forth that may have happened a few years back.

The night passed as we continued to drink and talk. We were just getting real cozy when she suddenly jumped up and said, "I'm tired. I'm going to bed." As she passed me, she asked, "Are you coming?"

# Chapter 9

# THE PARTY

THE PARTY BEING thrown by the principal owner and President of Wainwright Management on July 29 was going to be big. There was to be live music and a huge pig roast on the penthouse patio, attended by a bevy of gorgeous girls hired to entertain the many influential people invited.

"Will you be there?" I asked Yolanda.

"No, I have a previous engagement."

My mind raced with thoughts of meeting Dave Maier, principle stockholder of Wainwright Management. I asked Yolanda, who had the balls of a lion, to listen to my plan. "I'm working a night tour on that date. Could you call in to the fire department with a report of smoke coming from the roof of his building? No name will be necessary."

"Sure, okay, I'll do it!" Her eyes glistened with excitement. Then she added, "Don't forget, there's a possibility of seeing

Monique there. Wainwright uses a high end dating service for those parties and she'll most likely be one of the girls . I'll let her know what's going on."

This party was getting more and more interesting.

July 29th rolled around, and when I reported for duty I saw that to cover the shortage in the Chief's rank, Acting Battalion Chief Otto Ezold was going to be working. Otto, the Captain of E36 on 125th in Harlem, is a man you would not forget. Six foot six, over 250 pounds, he is the mayor of 125th Street because of his rapport with the community. He's a cigar smoking, scotch drinking affable guy who is totally at ease in his environment. Impressive and powerful, he has an incredible outgoing personality. If the community wanted a flag pole painted or a flag replaced, Otto would arrange for a tower ladder to reach the inaccessible places. Whenever he was Acting Battalion Chief on a day tour in our firehouse, he always took the Lexington Avenue subway from 125th to 85th Street, gear and all. I would then wind up driving him back to his quarters. Then we were off to the L&M, a bar on Lexington and 126th, Otto's favorite watering hole. I seldom made it home, ending up spending the night in the quarters of E36. I couldn't have been happier to see Big Otto working this night!

Sure enough, about 9:00 p.m. we get an alarm for smoke coming from a roof on 76th near 2nd Avenue. We were given an address and responded!

L13 took the first available elevator to the penthouse. E22 was just assembling near the elevator with the rolled up hose for a possible standpipe operation (water is pumped up to higher floors via internal building water pipes, and outlets on any of the landings can be used by the firemen). The chief, Big Otto, staying with the men of E22, told me to let him know what we had. It was usually a barbeque, a smoky chimney or the like, and can even be clothes dryer vents causing a smoky or steam condition.

We took the public elevator to the floor below the penthouse where another private elevator led directly into the penthouse apartment. This elevator is activated by the owners by either a number combination on the keypad or by a key. In an emergency our special Fire Department Key overrides the elevator systems, giving us access to all elevators including this private one. But knowing this is not an emergency I hit the buzzer, and from the intercom we get a "Who is it?" After I identify us and our purpose, the doors open and we are taken to the beautiful entry-way of this huge penthouse.

We are met by a man and a woman.

"I'm Dave Maier, the owner of this apartment, and this is my wife." In the background a party is going on that looks like a Broadway Show, with a band and lots of people dancing and drinking and having a ball. I know he is the principle owner of Wainwright and am very curious to see what he's like. With great friendliness and charm he announces it is his birthday celebration and knows why we are here. "This isn't the first time the fire department's been called to my barbeques, especially when the chefs have roasted pig on the menu…that can cause a lot of smoke."

I tell him that I have to eyeball the scene. My men and I continue onto the patio where everything appears perfectly normal. After checking we are careful not to soil his rugs. Seeing very delicate expensive rugs, we even removed our boots when re-entering from the patio. In appreciation of our courtesy he offers us a drink. After I tell him it is also my birthday his response is effusive, and I accept the drinks for me and my men. I call on the handi-talkie to Captain Otto, who is still waiting in the lobby, telling him that it's a barbeque and not a fire hazard. He tells me to take up when ready, and that he and E22 will return to the firehouse. I reply that there is a condition here that he might want to see. I want him to get a look at this party and also to have a drink. Having no doubt read this into my invitation, he replies in the negative, telling me to take my time, that he'll see me at quarters.

We have a drink, check out all the gorgeous girls, talk with the guests and are treated very cordially. Observing how friendly and gregarious Dave Maier is and knowing what I know about him, I have to resist my temptation to like him. I spot Monique in the crowd. We make eye contact but give no indication that we know each other. Dave sees me looking. "Good looking, eh Captain? She works for me in various capacities and is an okay broad."

We finish our drinks and are escorted to the penthouse elevator by Dave and his wife. She is a little cocktailed and I see she has an interest in one of our firemen, Jim Graham. She's all over him, and her husband doesn't seem to mind. After farewells we leave. It has been one interesting encounter which I will have to evaluate. During our conversation, Maier noted my age, and asked if I was considering retiring because they were looking for a consultant to oversee if their buildings were in conformity to current building laws, fire codes and the like. He gave me his business card and said if I was interested to come and see him. For some unknown reason he is interested in me. I wonder why. Guilt? I consider calling Elizabeth, the FBI agent, with this information.

# Chapter 10

# CARLOWS EAST

CECIL B. DeMILLE would have loved hanging out at Carlows East, named after the county in Ireland, with its rich pool of eclectic characters. You could find anyone from Dusty Dupont of the Dupont fortune to the supers and doormen of the expensive apartment complexes in Yorkville on the upper East Side. Doormen provide various services for their rich tenants and were always well taken care of with exceptional gratuities. At Christmas the gifts were huge. One fireman who became a doorman on 5th Avenue when he retired said his Christmas gifts were mind boggling. Supers were given free rent and a modest salary with all utilities paid. Any contractor work done in the old ten- and twenty-story buildings with huge spacious living areas had to go through the super, whose recommendation to hire specific contractors then went to the building manager. The supers' middleman services were also well compensated.

The rich tenants in this heavily populated area loved living on the upper East Side. The extremely good restaurants and fashionable bars with wealthy clientele were always crowded with talented, interesting people. Some loved the Irish entertainment on Friday and Saturday nights at Carlows. A great diversity of people, from cops to firemen to chefs, were all part of this great makeup. Almost anything could happen at Carlows.

One particular evening Jim Park, a fellow lieutenant, and I were relaxing with a few beers at Carlows after a busy day tour. Both of us had worked together in E218 in Brooklyn, had much in common and were talking about old times in the hectic days of the ghetto-heavy work in Brooklyn. Jim's other occupation was as proprietor of The Clay Pipe, a bar on Broadway and 12th Street. Two unusual nights were featured at the Clay Pipe. One was a key club where entering couples threw their keys in a circle and never left with their initial companions. The other night was for homosexuals who took over the whole place. Regulars were not there on these two nights. Jim did well, eventually lost his lease, but had a good run during this period where sexual inhibitions and restraints seemed to disappear.

As we are talking, a tall good looking brunette comes in about 8 o'clock and sits next to us. We offered her a drink, which she accepted and introduced herself as June. Conversation flowed free and loose and after some time, she turned to me and said seductively that she was heading to Plato's Retreat and would I like to come with her. Plato's Retreat in New York was a new happening and with the 1970's sexual revolution, it was going like gangbusters. AIDS had not arrived on the scene, so no one considered consequences and an awful lot of closeted people were coming out. I looked at Jim who said, "You're nuts if you don't." I accepted, ordered another drink and then we hailed a cab.

She had been to Plato's before and knew the routine. Men could only go in if escorted by a female. Females were more than welcome alone. We entered down a stairway two floors deep, so wide that four abreast could descend at the same time. She wouldn't allow me to pay for her so we went dutch. We were directed to a disrobing area, given lockers with a key and a towel for covering. She saw my nervousness, laughed, kissed me, took my hand and we headed for the first encounter. Her new attire revealed a great figure. My excitement was starting to show as we entered a large room where nude bodies were all over in various stages of sex, writhing and entwined with every orifice and erotic zone either filled, fondled or tasted.

"This room is a little too intense for me," she whispered, so it was on to the next area, a pool with nude couples and three-somes, some in the water, some on lounges with only one intent in mind: PLEASURE! It reminded me of accounts of the Roman orgies I'd read about. It was too much for me! I started to pro-trude from beneath the towel and ripped it off laying it on the tile floor, then laid down pulling June on top of me. She was very strong and her sensual gyrations were intense. I held on for a great ride. We reached an explosive, extremely wet orgasm and I wondered where all the waves of fluid had come from. No one even noticed: we were just a small part of an incredible scene.

When finally we jumped into the shallow end of the pool, I told June I couldn't swim and laughingly related how our swim coach in high school, "The Commander," had insisted we swim without bathing suits during swim classes. I never adjusted to the public nudity, so I skipped swim periods and, being an inner city kid, I never learned to swim. Later I learned that "The Commander" had come out of the closet.

We lounged for a while taking in all the scenes. I get excited again and she led me to another location of private and semi-private rooms. We took a private room and grabbed each other, making indulgent love again. After a fruit drink (no alcohol was served on the premises), it was time for a little nap. Half asleep, we groped each other.

Much later we decide to leave, hungry and looking for a place to eat. We find a really good pizza place which served cold beer and wine, and while we ate she asked if I'd had a good time. "It was a once in a lifetime experience! If I didn't like it, I wouldn't be normal. Plus I thought you were great company!" I gushed.

We finished and hailed two cabs. She gave me her telephone number and we were off, she to the Village, me back to Carlows to relish and relive my evening. After two martinis my brain did its usual levitation from its setting of muck and mire and with tonight's experience, it really was somewhere in outer space.

# Chapter 11

# MASHED POTATOES

TODAY I WAS looking forward to the activity planned for tomorrow on my nine-hour layover between night tours. It was our scheduled visit to McDonald House on 86th and Second Avenue. The firehouse was abuzz with preparation for the visit.

John Thomsian, our resident amateur magician, had arrived with my daughter Mary, who had become his assistant. John had been putting on shows for us and for other firehouses for Christmas parties, picnics and any occasion where children came with their families. Once a hobby, John's magic had gotten quite good and he had trained Mary to assist him. They were a good team and were starting to get a reputation.

Food preparation was completed and we headed for McDonald House near noon. Most of us walked the two blocks and were there when the tower ladder arrived with its cast.

Watching them, I reflected on the generous hearts of most firemen; it made me proud.

The children housed there all have cancer of some type and McDonald's has set up facilities like this throughout the country to make things a little easier for them and their families. Being together with their families while receiving their treatment and having the company of other children in the same boat is a big factor in recovery.

Last December, L13 and E22 went to the Ronald McDonald House for Christmas with our own Santa Claus, fire fighter Tom Glynn. We left quarters with Tom dressed as Santa riding in the Tower Ladder Bucket, surrounded by gifts for the kids. Ample Tom was a beautiful sight as we traveled to McDonald House with many cheers and waves from pedestrians along the way. When we arrived Tom was hoisted to the roof of the building and descended on the interior stairs to the dining area, along with his elves carrying the gifts.

For the occasion we brought along a turkey dinner we'd cooked in the firehouse. It included all the trimmings, including an army-sized pot of mashed potatoes. After serving dinner, gifts were handed out to the kids and afterwards we put on a magic show which included John Thomasian, with my daughter Mary as his assistant. They were really good at making doves appear and a rabbit disappear. Dan Garvey played the bagpipes and Jules Keitt came in with Victor the Constrictor draped around his neck, to squeals of surprise from the children. The sing-along finale brought the day to a great conclusion. We all walked to the front street and watched as Tom was taken from the roof with the Tower Ladder

A thank-you letter from the truly great McDonald House

staff included drawings and comments from the kids. To our amazement all the letters had an inclusive rave about the mashed potatoes. They just couldn't get enough of them.

So now, by popular demand, we are going to do a repeat performance in July. Along with our usual contingent there will be an abundance of mashed potatoes, with two huge meat-loaves replacing the turkey. The sauce for the meat loaves is being made with our exclusive secret recipe (Hunts tomato sauce with mashed, cooked sweet potatoes dissolved into it). I couldn't wait to see the kids dig in to our culinary delights. Feelings like that cling to your heart for the rest of your life.

Something else I'll never forget is a freezing fire that happened on one of the coldest nights I can recall. In late January, E218 is "special called" to a third alarm for a fire in a twenty-family four story building. On arrival we found it was already in a "defensive attack stage" due to the building collapse potential. It was now an outside fire. Two tower ladders supplying water by pumpers were operating their heavy water guns onto the roof area with engine companies operating hand-held hose lines into the windows. In fires like this, fatigue sets in very quickly because of the ice build-up on the men and their heavy equipment.

The chief in charge ordered us to try to take a hose line up to the top floor by a rear fire escape to extinguish a pocket of fire that the outside streams couldn't get to. He mentioned that the fire escapes were icy: we were ordered to use extreme caution; if it turned out to not be possible, we were not to take measures that could cause injuries.

We stretched a line to the rear and discovered the fire escape covered in ice from the tower ladder sprays. Cautiously we made our way to the top floor. Our helmets, coats and boots were soon caked with ice and we kept moving to prevent too much build-up.

When we get to the top floor the fire was visible and accessible to a hose stream from the window, but we couldn't open the frozen nozzle and had to slide the hose line into the fire to melt the ice. The chief sent orders through his handi-talkie to the tower ladders to not operate the water guns into the building's rear exposure number three (the rear of the building.) We operated into the window and extinguished all visible fire. We looked up at one of the tower ladders operating from above the roof's rear exposure and saw what looked like a prehistoric monster in a foggy smoky swamp, with a long neck to the bucket: two firemen operating the water guns looked like the head of the monster. The eerie looking, penetrating high-powered light beams along with the powerful water stream spitting into the fire completed the monster picture.

We notified the chief of our successful operation and were told to leave the hose line there, where it could be safely retrieved when the weather warmed up. "Good job," he said, "report to me in front of the fire building."

Slowly we made our very dangerous descent. The chief told us to take up, but advised us that one of the neighborhood families had invited all firemen at the scene to go to their house to warm up if we wanted. We entered the couple's home with ice clinging to us and saw that they'd spread paper and towels on the floor. They appreciated what we'd done and offered us shots of brandy and whiskey. We were overwhelmed by their hospitality and compassion.

A few weeks later after finishing a night tour, we decided to take a bouquet of flowers to the kind couple to show our appreciation. Three of us went to our local florist. After telling him the story, he made up a really beautiful arrangement.

We knocked on their door and the woman answered. She smiled at the flowers and we notice a room full of people sitting in a group. She explained that the big tall impressive looking gentlemen, her husband, had died a few days ago and that the group was heading to the funeral home and burial. Stunned and sad, we offered this angel our condolences and she graciously offered us cake and coffee, trying to make us feel better. We noticed that they were using the wrong type of coffee for their big coffee urn. Sometime later, the women sent a thank you card to the firehouse, thanking us for the flowers and coffee. The men had taken 10 bags of coffee (the correct type for her coffee maker) from our commissary back to her house.

Here's another instance of firemen's generosity:

The Federal Government had established a Dialogue Program with the intent of improving community relations between ghetto neighborhood youths and the police and fire departments. This program consisted of eight teams of six neighborhood youths with one fireman in charge of each team. By city school buses, all 48 youths were taken on four trips. One trip was to the Phoenix House of alcohol and substance abuse on Hart Island in Long Island Sound, another to Washington, D.C. to government and educational places such as the Smithsonian Institution, and The U.S. Mint. Another trip was to Roseland Ranch in upstate New York, for barbeques, horseback rides and nature hikes, and the last excursion was to the Fire Department Training Center on Welfare Island in the East River to familiarize the boys with a fireman's job. At the end of the day each team had to drag a dummy from one of the smoke-filled training buildings, without masks, with the winning team given a cash prize of $60.00.

With all the activities on these outing — soft ball games, ping pong matches, excursions, eating and bus travel time — the ultimate goal of the program was to have the groups be with and have a dialogue with the firemen. There were many questions: "Why do firemen break windows, put holes in roofs, tear down walls and use so much water after the fires are out? Don't they care about the people living there?" they asked. We explained that we break windows and open roofs to remove poisonous smoke and extreme heat from the buildings because it's the smoke and heat that kills most victims, not the actual fire. The washing down after the visible fire is out is done to make sure the fire is completely out and not hiding somewhere.

Slowly the wall of mistrust between the kids and the firemen came down. We got to know each other and soon laughter and good natured kidding were part of the dialogue. We treated them with respect and received the same in return. Leaving the Washington, D.C. hotel, the manager complimented them on their excellent behavior in contrast to a recent high school football team there on a trip which was out of control and damaged some of the hotel.

After our last trip my six youths were dropped off at my firehouse. Four lived locally and could walk home safely. Two lived much further away in Queens, in a housing project, Rochdale Village, which was a high crime area. Finding out they had no transportation other then public, I offered to drive them home. Approaching Rochdale, the boys told me not to drive into the Village because it could be dangerous for me, and to stay on the main road. Before they got out of the car one boy, Santos, asked, "Can I ask you something personal?" "Of Course," I answered.

"Why are you doing this, what's in it for you?" After thinking about it I replied, "I have a son just about your age and if some-day you had a chance meeting with him, I'd hope you could treat each other with no prejudged feelings." There was silence for awhile and then the reply, "I understand."

Remembering these three events, I was again amazed at the emotional scope of most firemen. They were tough enough to deal with brutal fires; brave enough to risk their lives to rescue fire victims; generous enough to use their free time to reach out to those in need. Great guys. I felt pride to be among them.

# Chapter 12

# THE TUMULTUOUS 1960'S AND 70'S

I JOINED THE FIRE department in 1958 after a 1952–3 stint in Korea and five years on the police department. I stayed for 33 years, until 1991, and remember the 1960s and 70s as the crazy years.

In the early 1950s, before the drug culture arrived full blast in the states, my brother went often to The Cotton Club in Harlem and never had to worry about taking public transportation. The subways were safe then, but the drug culture changed all that. Uncertainty and fear caused by the pressures of the cold war; Kennedy's assassination; the coming of the Vietnam War; unemployment (particularly in the low income sector), all contributed to the unrest and civil disobedience in the City as well as the rest of the country. The City government was inept and totally mishandled negotiations with civil service unions.

One particular labor union blunder remains vivid in my

mind. City labor negotiators had given the New York City detectives union a five percent differential raise above all other uniformed forces. Unfortunately, the negotiators didn't know there was a piggyback clause on all uniformed forces contracts. At a cost of over $200 Million, all the other City unions received the same raise. In addition, Mayor Lindsey had to deal with Mike Quill, president of the Transport Workers Union. The crafty, wily, knowledgeable leader of the TWU, took "Mr. Lindsley" and the City to the cleaners. The corruption and mismanagement of welfare and social programs also had an effect on the City. Mayor Beame, the next mayor after Lindsey, knew that governing the City was an insurmountable task but applied for the job anyway and took all the hits like the tough little man he was.

In the 1960s while serving as a lieutenant at E218 in Brooklyn , I saw many things totally out of control. Welfare was unmanageable. A local postman told me how he often delivered three or four welfare checks to the same person, same address with slightly different name spellings. No investigation was required to get welfare; just a signed affidavit requesting benefits gave you eligibility. Welfare recipient unions were proposed, demanding rights and more compensation. Surely the inmates were taking over the asylum.

Storefront job and food programs were unsupervised and thievery was rampant. Unused food for the poor was thrown out, to make sure there was room for the distributors to deliver automatic full loads to the storefronts. The distributors paid off the operators of these humanitarian storefronts for their services. Desks, chairs, typewriters, paper supplies and other office equipment sat in other storefronts and never fulfilled their intent to train the jobless.

This mess was not the blame of the poverty stricken: it was the rampant corruption, the mismanagement, the arson for profit that all contributed to the 1960s –70's chaos. Not a pretty picture but that's the way it was. I had always thought that civil disobedience was the main cause: not true. It was only one of the many factors that led to the frustration of the poor.

In 1968, a year after I was promoted to lieutenant and not yet assigned to a company, I was covering a vacation in L147 in Brooklyn. The war in Vietnam and the lack of jobs were causing rumbles of discontent in the poor ghetto areas.

Harlem exploded that summer into a full scale riot and civil disobedience with the assassination of Martin Luther King. Looting, burning and shooting from roof tops made it a war zone. The department had a plan for this and staging areas at certain firehouses were set up for all the fire control teams needed to respond to fires and, while attempting to put out the fires, to do as much as they could to control the savage situation.

We were one team sent from Brooklyn to Harlem to be part of the control teams sent from all over the city. Teams consisted of a police car in the lead with two engine companies, a ladder company, and a police car to protect the rear of the convoy.

E58 and L26, with wide Lenox Avenue in front of their quarters, was one of the staging areas. At night, with lights out and no sirens, teams stealthily slipped into the staging area. The fire department did what they could to control the situation, but it was no good: it was out of control. Some teams couldn't even enter blocks that were roaring with fire. The people there were shooting from the roofs, making entry to the block untenable. The riots ran their course and after several days they calmed down — more from fatigue than anything else — leaving a scorched desolate landscape. It looked like pictures of war-torn Europe during World War II.

What sticks in my mind about this chaotic time was the remarkable job the host firehouses did in feeding the many cops and firemen temporarily attached to them, sometimes as many as 300 at a time. They worked away in their kitchens, using big heavy pots to cook hams, potatoes and vegetables. Somehow they secured picnic tables from nearby parks and the apparatus floors became big dining halls. In groups of 50, all team members were served great meals.

The men of E58 and L26 (the Fire Factory) did an unbelievable job in their white aprons. John Sinino, head chef and boss of this whole dining operation, later wrote a best selling cook book, *Fire House Meals.*

Starting in 1978–79, Koch slowly brought the city around. He said he would prosecute arson aggressively and warned arsonists that they would be severely punished. He put efficient non-political people in important city positions and conditions gradually began to change. Establishing rapport with the city labor unions; treating everyone fairly without bending to pressure groups; giving tax breaks to big corporations as an incentive to return to the city, initiated a positive impact. Earlier in 1977, while working on an assignment in a high-rise office building downtown, I noted that one in three office spaces were vacant. At Melon's, a very upscale restaurant on the upper East Side, I got into a chance conversation with a young real estate agent. I mentioned the vacant office spaces. He replied that in two years the office real estate market would go through the roof and there would be almost none available. How right he was and I often wondered who that realtor was.

No one can truly assess the damage that out-of-control arson had on the public and the fire department. The hardships to the public, the workloads for our uniformed forces, was catastrophic and costly in money and lives. It was not uncommon for fire units in the dense ghetto areas to respond to eight to ten thousand alarms in a year, and a few units had even higher alarm responses. The many hours of fighting structural fires in occupied buildings took its toll on the fire companies and the loss to families living there were extremely cruel and disheartening.

But somehow the City survived until Koch began the reforms, and so did the fire department and its men. I always thought that Koch was the greatest mayor New York City ever had.

# Chapter 13

# WAINWRIGHT HALL

WAINWRIGHT HALL IS one of the resplendent new queens of Manhattan, built in the early 1970s on the wealthy Upper East Side. Its exquisite forty stories is elegantly adorned in white brick, the façade accented with balconies. It boasts a sumptuous entrance which swallows guests into an expansive stunning lobby. Voices echo in its vastness; glistening chandeliers float high above, delivering warm light to rich oriental rugs below.

Imported dark leather sofas with comfortable club chairs are available for weary feet or those who just wish to sit and admire. With spacious soundproof apartments and the most modern appurtenances, Wainwright Hall is one of the newest and most desired buildings among the urbane Upper East Side.

Blocks away a sister building, Curzon House, is a sublime replica. The next third sister, embryonic and yet to be named, is fussed over on an architectural scale model in a prominent section of two lobbies. All three buildings were conceived in evil acts.

The unfortunate occupants of the buildings which formerly stood on these buildings' foundations were forced out, many of them violently. If these tenants were foolish enough to refuse onerous financial terms, arson and harassment were inflicted by despicable supers. We know that water leaks, broken pipes, lack of heat, purported "building improvement projects" which kept tenants up morning and night — all ultimately left unfinished — were carried out with cunning perseverance. Such a heartless blitzkrieg was pursued by Wainwright Management, to make way for their three luxury buildings.

On my next set of 9:00 to 6:00 day tours, I left word for Elizabeth, the FBI agent, with information on how organized crime might be involved in the arson fires. I also wanted to tell her of my contrived meeting with David Maier at his penthouse birthday party.

Elizabeth returned my call at noon. I told her about the meeting with Dave and Yolanda's information about Mafia involvement with Danny O, the arsonist.

I get the typical FBI response: closemouthed. They've been aware of 'some organized crime involvement' in the arson investigation but had no information yet that would pin it down.

"We might possibly squeeze other areas of investigations of organized crime for a lead in this investigation," Elizabeth offered. About the meeting with Dave Maier, she asked me to call her if any useful situation presented itself. "Thanks, Gene, I'll keep in touch," she ended, leaving me feeling unfulfilled.

The very next day I have a scheduled A.F.I.D. (apparatus field inspection duty), 9:30 to 1:00 p.m. Our unit, a Tower Ladder, is not used for building inspections because of various operations where a tower ladder must be available immediately. L13 switched personnel with E22 and took their unit, a Pumper, for the inspections of buildings in our district

I decide to inspect Wainwright Management's hi-rise residence building on First Avenue and 80th Street, Wainwright Hall though it's not a normal thing to go out of our regularly scheduled block-by-block sequence. I notify Battalion 10 that I'm going to deviate from the schedule because I want to familiarize some of the new members with fire operations in hi-rise residential buildings. He gives me the OK and notes that a possible training class might be useful for all members.

After coffee in the morning, I assemble the members for our 9:30 A.F.I.D. building inspections. The men put on their uniform hats and semi-dress shirts, the required uniform. Appearance goes a long way toward creating the desired effect of professionalism. The doorman, knowing our purpose, says he'll notify the building manager who is also the required Fire Safety Director. In the event of a fire, he is to have an elevator bank at our disposal. We have fire department keys that operate the elevators, overriding all other calls. Also part of his job is to follow the fire safety plan posted on all floors and enforce it when the building is to be evacuated. He has taken a required course on this and is licensed.

We wait in the plush lobby until Jim Spencer, the Fire Safety Director and building manager, arrives and introduces himself. I give him my card and tell him it's our annual building inspection. We have a check list, a Standard Form of Orders that starts at the roof and works down. The firemen take a handi-talkie with them and head for the roof. My handi-talkie keeps me in constant contact with them in case we get called to a fire. Mine is a roving position between them and our chauffeur in the fire truck outside who also has a handi-talkie. I go to Jim Spencer's office where he produces all the permits and certificates required by law. They're all current. I ask a few questions and get accurate and knowledgeable replies. I then tell him I will walk around and check the perimeter of the building.

I check elevators, garbage compactor systems, self-closing devices on doors, all signs for Fire Deptartment services, and the like. After a thorough inspection my men will meet me at the Director's office. The whole procedure takes about an hour and a half. Any violations will be written up and the Director will be given a time limit for compliance. Some violations, such as locked egresses, a very serious condition, result in an immediate summons.

When I return to the office my men are there and who appears but Dave Maier himself. His manager had called him and he wanted to see how things were. Aside from a few minor violations everything seems in order. Maier shakes my hand and says it is a pleasure to see me again . . . just what I was hoping would happen. Mentioning that he had one other hi-rise building and another in the works, he repeated what he'd offered at his party: he was looking for a coordinator to oversee that his building operations conform to all building codes, health codes, labor laws, fire regulations, hi-rise building codes and preventative maintenance; if I was interested I'd be that man.

"I hadn't considered retiring but it's time to give it some thought," I cordially replied.

"We could establish a part time arrangement until you make up your mind." he counter-offered, and asked if I would please call his office and make an appointment to meet with him, bringing my resume.

"I'll give that some serious consideration," I said.

My men looked very professional, did a good job and were impressive. I left on a good note and a firm handshake. I wondered what the circumstance of his building in the works would entail. Would they use the procedures they'd used in other buildings to remove stubborn tenants? I wished that I could get closer cooperation with the FBI but knew they didn't work that way. I'll have to go to the proposed site and check the mood and opinions of the neighborhood.

It will be important to keep a straight face, hiding my disgust at the greed and inhumanity Wainwright Management shows toward people.

On my return to quarters I find a note that Elizabeth has called. I return her call, wondering if there's any progress from their investigation. She asks if I can come to FBI headquarter on 69th Street for an interview with her and Bill Wilson, the agent who had set up our first meeting. We agree on an 11:00 a.m. meeting at their office on Friday, three days hence.

On Friday I show up at the FBI Headquarters, a huge 22-story building that takes up the whole block facing Second Avenue. Ironically, just after I'd being assigned to L13 in July of 1977, we had a fire on this very roof. They had been replacing the roof and the building materials had somehow caught fire. The tar and other highly flammable materials made for a huge spectacular fire which looked more dangerous than it was, though it did cause the lights and elevators to go out of service. The 22-story climb in darkened hallways with our heavy equipment had made it a tough ascent to the roof. I resolved then and there to give up smoking. Unfortunately, that only lasted six months.

I checked the building directory for Agent Elizabeth Peters' office. It was listed under Arson Investigations, Room 1010. At the visitors desk I call and am told they're waiting for me. It's a friendly informal meeting; coffee is offered and I accept. FBI agent Bill Wilson, Elizabeth's supervisor, asks if I've received any further information from Yolanda. I told them no, I hadn't gotten any thing more because I can't get in touch with her. Evidently they must have checked her background, found out she was a player and thought her information might be useful.

I told them about my meeting with the owner of Wainwright Management at his penthouse birthday party and about my purposeful inspection of Wainwright Hall. I mentioned his job offer to become an advisor and trouble shooter concerning rules and regulations for his buildings; that I told him I wasn't sure I wanted to retire and his counter-offer to take me on part-time until I made a decision. There was silence as Wilson and Elizabeth absorbed this.

"Are you aware that this could be an unwise and dangerous decision for you?" asks Wilson.

"No more dangerous than the job I do everyday and, more importantly, I don't want them to get away with what they've done and will continue to do. But if you can show me some progress on your investigation I'll reconsider."

"We're making some headway but as our regulations note, this information can't be shared unless approved by higher-ups. We'll look into this possibility and keep in touch."

The meeting ends cordially.

Agent Peters walks me to the elevator and with genuine concern takes my hand and gently asks if I'm getting too emotionally involved. With her family background in the fire department, I sense a kindred spirit and thank her for her concern.

# Chapter 14

# FIRST UNIT CITATION

WHILE I WORKED as a covering officer waiting for a permanent assignment, I always noted the unit citations posted on the walls near the firehouse entrance. I was dismayed that L13 and E22 had none.

Now I know that the uptown "Fire Factory" (L26 and E58) and "The Harlem Hilton" (L28 and E69) were great companies, and that all their unit citations were well deserved. If a golfer plays five times a week and another plays once a week, surely the busier golfer's skills would be more honed than the once-a-week player's. But 20 to 30 citations to zero was way out of line. One of the advantages of working in a busy company was that the officers and chiefs were willing to extend themselves to show appreciation for a job well done. But writing up a unit citation or a personal medal is very time consuming, so often well deserving acts go unrecognized.

In our job there is no bonus for work well done; there is no compensatory time off for incentive. The only way to show appreciation is in the personnel write-up. Most important, a write-up awards merit points on a test for promotion. Three points is maximum and a quarter-point is the minimum. Adding these to a final average can mean the difference between getting promoted from fireman to lieutenant and on up the ladder.

Here's how we got our first:

On my next set of night tours, Battalion Chief Glynn was covering an open slot in the 10th Battalion. I knew him from Brooklyn when he was a captain. That night we get a call at 11:00 p.m. for a fire on 82nd Street between 2nd and 3rd Avenues. We rolled into the block. Nothing showed except people on the street waving their arms and yelling. "Where's the fire?" I shouted at them and they indicated the third floor rear. "Are there people in the apartment?" I asked, and they replied "No, they're all in the street." I took this into account but, as always, didn't depend on the accuracy of street information.

While E22 took a hydrant and stretched a line we, the forcible entry team, headed for the third floor. The fire was in the rear left side apartment at the end of the hallway. The closed door showed blistering from the heat and fire.

We opened the unlocked door gradually . . . an intense fire was showing, so we closed the door and waited for E22 to bring the hose line. We checked the next door apartment and discovered an old couple in a state of panic. The hallway was filled with firemen, smoke and heat so we took the couple to their apartment's rear fire escape. My roof man handi-talkied that the roof was vented. We knew that would relieve the hall from some smoke and heat, but also knew that when the on-fire door to the apartment was opened for the water line, a rush of smoke and heat would enter the hall.

From the fire escape we notified the chief that we had the couple with us and, due to their age and immobility, we felt the fire escape was a safe place for the present. My outside vent man secured the front two apartments, found no one is in them, and notified the chief. Then he joined me on the fire escape.

My roof man was coming down the rear fire escape to our position and moving to the other side of the fire escape. He entered the rear window of the fire apartment, heard the engine line at work and initiated a search. He again reported his actions to the chief. Leaving the outside vent man with the old couple, I took the forcible entry fireman and headed back to the entrance of the blazing apartment. We filed in behind the engine line which was directing their stream on the fire. We searched all the adjoining rooms, checked the fire room and notified the Chief that the primary search for victims was complete. A secondary search by another company completed the search. L39 did this, and I notified the Chief that the secondary search was complete, and that the engine company had extinguished all visible fire.

The Battalion Chief headed up to the scene and checked our work, acknowledging a job well done by all units. The handi-talkies had been crackling with accurate fire reports. We examined for any fire extension in the ceilings and behind walls, checked the floor above and in adjoining apartments, etc. E22 completed its wash down with the hose to make sure all fire was out and then we took up and headed for the street.

Standing by the fire trucks, we found Battalion Chief Glynn and the Deputy Chief of the Third Division talking about how pleased they were with the operation. I requested a unit citation for L13 and E22. Chief Glynn said to write it up; he would endorse it. The Deputy Chief nodded his agreement. I congratulated our company for a job well done. All communications had been on time and accurate; it was a very efficient and complete operation. I rode back to the firehouse, envisioning our first unit citation on our wall.

# Chapter 15

# THE BEAUTIFUL BROWNSTONE

LIKE MOST FIREMEN, I appreciate beautiful buildings. I see a lot of them on our inspections. One I'm particularly fond of is a lavish one on Manhattan's Upper East Side, a sturdy brownstone. It's similar to the brownstones scattered throughout city neighborhoods. This one was built at the turn of the century and now, over 75 years later, it remains one of the city's most desirable residences, especially since its new owner gave it a beautiful face lift.

Spreads in architectural and interior design magazines extol its solid limestone exterior which has replaced deteriorating loose brick and crumbling mortar joints which have been repaired and repointed by expert masons. Decades of soot that obscured medieval cornices and gargoyles have been washed away. Pane glass windows and doorframes have been replaced and restored, copper gutters and black wrought iron fences have been renewed. This brownstone is again what it once was, a classic of the ages.

The home's interior was redesigned with an exciting new look. From the expansive vestibule, rising three floors to a ceiling with an octagonal stained glass skylight, a sparkling crystal chandelier hangs from the center of the skylight. The new owner spared no expense installing an elevator for easy access to all floors and the basement. The walls are adorned with renaissance paintings and beautiful statues. It feels like a museum. A regal staircase leads to the second floor balcony which overlooks the entrance. This floor contains bedrooms and a sitting room The stairs continue to the third floor balcony which has additional bedrooms and a gymnasium. The first floor under the balconies contains the kitchen, formal dining area, library and living room and overlooks a beautifully landscaped rear garden. The renovation surpasses this brownstone's original opulence, but now it is on fire!

* * *

We roll in. E39 has a hose line stretched to the entrance door and L16 is putting their aerial ladder to the roof. Since this building stands alone, access to the roof is only by aerial ladder. Until the roof is open, visibility to the inside conditions is zero. After L16 gets the roof open, the gases and heat lift enough to show a very heavy volume of smoke emanating from the second floor in the rear of the building.

As visibility improves, E39 moves its hose line up the stairs and discovers a roaring fire in a bedroom. They enter and start extinguishment. L16 is checking the other rooms on this floor for any occupants. My L13's area of responsibility is the third floor above the fire. The firemen are to search for occupants, vent windows, and check for fire extension as L16 does on the second floor.

My chauffeur, John Thomasian, spots an occupant waving at a smoky second floor window on the left side of the building. He takes a portable ladder into the alleyway, climbs to the window, stabilizes, and assures a heavy older man on the window ledge. In the meantime Feilmoser, our roof man, has taken a roof rope via L16's aerial ladder to the roof.

After a visible search looking over the perimeter of the building, Feilmoser spots the occupant with Tomasian at the second floor window. Feilmoser throws one end of the rope from the roof to the street, secures his end around the chimney, connects it to his harness and single-slides down to the window.

I get a handi-talkie message from Thomasian asking me what action he and Feilmoser should take with the man they have on the window sill of the "exposure two side, "second floor", (a building has four sides. Going clockwise from the front, the left side is exposure two). They feel that using the ladder for descent could be very difficult and dangerous for the older man. I reply to hold him at the window since it now looks like the fire has been extinguished and smoke is clearing in the interior. L16 hears my message, locates the room and is now also at the window with the occupant and reports that in a little while he can be taken down the interior stairs.

When all positions are secure, we head for the street for a welcomed break. I meet Thomasian and Feilmoser and congratulate them on their quick thinking and good job. I then seek out the chief in command of the fire to tell him of this outstanding act and that I would like to write them up for an award. I'm surprised to receive a very sour smirk and a reply that he thinks it was pretty routine, but he adds that if I feel it has merit, I should forward a Meritorious Act Report. I know that, with this negative reaction, his endorsement will be lukewarm and it will go nowhere, once again exemplifying the unfairness and favoritism in the system. I forward it anyway.

# Chapter 16

# YOLANDA'S DAUGHTER

THE DAY AFTER the brownstone fire, Yolanda calls to ask if it's okay to stop by the firehouse with her daughter Monica who has crushes on firemen. I tell her we have nothing scheduled and it would be a good time to visit.

A half hour later Yolanda and her beautiful daughter arrive. The house watchman notifies me that I have visitors. I meet them at the front door and invite them to the kitchen. Monica, 17 years old, is checking out every fireman she sees and is loving it. One of my new firemen, Larry McMahon, brings them a soda and coffee and is a very gracious host. Afterwards, I show them around the firehouse. They love "Victor the Constrictor" who lives in my office. They ask lots of questions about the trucks, equipment and firehouse routine. I walk them out and see then off.

An hour later I get a call from Yolanda telling me how much they enjoyed the firehouse tour. They were now visiting at Monique's (Yolanda's friend whose furniture I had helped move). Laughing, she tells me that Monica was smitten with Larry McMahon and asks if we would be interested in a dinner one night at Francesco's on 92nd and First Avenue. In the background I hear Monique giggling and yelling, "Find a fireman for me too!" The girl is a knockout; I instantly think of Jerry Guilfoyle. I tell Yolanda I'll see if I can put something together. When Jerry relieves me that night, I tell him the story. He, Larry and I agree that it could be a fun encounter. Next morning I call Yolanda to say that Jerry and Larry are interested in a triple date at Francesco's. "We've checked our schedules and commitments. Would Friday night, two days from now, be good?" She confirms and we agree on 7:00 o'clock.

Friday night Jerry, Larry and I walk over to Francesco's. The ladies are waiting in front of the restaurant. Monica ogles Larry; Monique, I can tell, likes what she sees in Jerry and it's a smooth start to a delightful dinner. After a couple of hours of enjoying a good Chianti wine, Monica (who was drinking Virgin Mary's) asks if she can take Larry for a ride in their new Lincoln. She has a learners permit and with Larry a licensed driver, all bases are covered.

A half hour later Larry returns, looking a little shaken. He asks if he can talk to me outside. He relates how Monica had sideswiped a car on a turn and did slight damage to a rear fender of her car. She was shaken up, knowing what her mother's reaction would be. "No damage to the car's bumper she hit," Larry says, "and the Lincoln had only a slight indentation. I could push it out with the car-jack and no one would know the difference. So we opened the trunk and when I lifted a blanket to get at the jack, I saw two automatic pistols! I right away thought about my job . . . being a probationary fireman, if a cop had showed up I could've lost my job. So I quickly closed the trunk and told Monica I'd walk back to the restaurant. She drove back on her own, found a parking place and waited for me."

Larry tells me he wants to return to the firehouse, which I can readily understand. He says goodby to Monica and is off. Monica has to now go in and tell the story to her mother who reacts just as expected. Finally Yolanda calms down and we stay a while longer before calling it a night. Jerry says he'll walk Monique the four blocks to her apartment and they're off, both seeming to have enjoyed an otherwise great evening. We decide to leave the car parked and I walk Yolanda and Monica to their apartment a few blocks away. Yolanda wants me to come up and stay awhile but I tell her I want to go back to the firehouse to see Larry. She understands, but I can see she's disappointed.

At the firehouse the house watchman tells me that Larry has walked over to Carlows and that he looked upset. I head over and join Larry at the bar. We go over the whole incident and his concern about losing his job. He tells me, "Cap, I'd rather not do this again."

After this date I didn't see Yolanda again. I called her Ossining, New York number and it was no longer in service. I checked at her burned-out apartment, now being renovated; talked to the super who informed me she was no longer staying at the temporary apartment and that he hadn't heard from her. Where was Yolanda?

# Chapter 17

# JOB INTERVIEW

THE CRISP AUTUMN weather has arrived. I call Dave Maier to tell him I have a resume and to ask if we can set up a meeting since I'm off the following Monday and Tuesday, the last week in October. We agree on Monday at 10 a.m in his management office on 56th Street just off Lexington. That morning I drive to the firehouse from Long Beach and park, then take the Lexington subway to 59th Street, just a few blocks from his office.

I arrive fifteen minutes early and his efficient looking secretary, JoAnn, directs me to his office waiting room. At exactly ten, Dave opens his office door and greets me with a broad smile and a firm handshake. For a brief moment, it occurs to me that I might have a hard time hiding my intense disgust for him. Over coffee, he also points out the beautiful fall day while eying my resume. I've put my experience in short, concise chronological order: five years on the New York City Police Department, twenty years on the New York City Fire Department, and five years in the U.S. Coast Guard Reserve. He is interested in my reserve duty with the Coast Guard.

I explain that haphazard oil spillages and chemical waste dumped into water tributaries polluted the waters in and around New York State so badly that fish and wildlife became rare. In 1973, the U.S. Government passed the Clean Water Act. The Coast Guard didn't have the manpower to enforce it however, so where else to go but New York City's Police and Fire Departments? We were given the rank of Petty Officer First Class and after an intense two week training course we were sent out in Coast Guard vehicles to inspect oil depots, chemical plants near waterways, and cargo vessels shipping in and out of New York. In just five years there had been vast improvement in water quality and fish were reappearing in the Hudson and East Rivers. It was truly an accolade to the efficiency and dedication of the United States Coast Guard.

After more small talk, Dave suggests we take a ride over to Wainwright Hall at 80th and First Avenue to discuss job expectations. When we get there, we see his fire safety director, Jim Spencer, who supervises and enforces the regulations of the building codes pertaining to hi-rise office and residence buildings more than ten stories high. Local Law Five of the building code was written in 1975 to correct serious flaws in hi-rise building construction. I also point out to Dave that while recovering from an illness I was put on light duty for a while. I was assigned to the office of Deputy Chief Sid Ifsin, the architect who, along with the building department, wrote Local Law Five.

Local Law Five sited serious building fires in Korea and Brazil which caused many needless deaths because the skyscrapers were built without consideration to smoke and fire extension. Most notorious were the defects in the outer wall "skins" of the buildings which weren't connected to the interior concrete floors. Although the buildings' steel beams were connected to the outer skin, there were deadly pockets of space between the steel beams which left vertical voids running the full height of the building! This was the biggest cause of the fires spreading and the consequent deaths in the Korean and Brazilian catastrophes.

In Manhattan, such a disaster occurred in 1970 at One New York Plaza, located less than a mile from where the World Trade Center was being built. The fire's searing heat almost caused a total collapse of the 50-story building; intensified heat through the voids just about disintegrated the building's concrete blocks to bare steel girders, causing some of them to twist. Compounding the problem were serious flaws in fire-proofing the steel girders. Cost-cutting inferior quality fire-proofing material had been sprayed on the girders at the steel yards and much of it was known to have come off en route to the construction sites.

The fire at One New York Plaza started in a carpet wholesale showroom which covered most of one of the upper floors. Because of the openness of the showroom floor the fire raced through and engulfed the entire floor, creating heat of 1200 degrees and twisting the steel beams that were made bare by the intensity of the fire. Since there were no walls in this showroom to contain a fire, compartmentation of floors became mandatory. This and other factors contributed to the Local Law Five and building code changes.

I gave Dave a quick overview of possible problems — potential shoddy construction in the initial construction, for example;

contractors not properly closing holes made during interim repairs; maintenance and enforcement of use of self-closing devices on all doors to prevent winds from whipping through and hence spreading any fires. "Preventive maintenance is more cost efficient in the long run," I advised.

"Yes," Dave replied, "these potential problems are to be addressed."

We agreed that I would take the job on a trial basis, working once a week. At the end of the year, in two months, I would make my decision whether to accept the job permanently and retire from the Fire Department. I would be off the next two Mondays and would report to Jim Spencer. We talked salary and I was very pleased with his offer. Dave offered me a ride to the firehouse but on such a beautiful day I wanted to walk and use the time to do some hard thinking.

Midway through the cavernous lobby of Wainwright Hall I hear, "Hi Gene!' behind me and who is it but Monique, Yolanda's friend. She gives me a giant hug and asks. "What are you doing here?"

"I might take a part time consultant job with Wainwright Management," I explain.

She is delighted and asks if I've seen Yolanda. I tell her about my attempts to call and her disconnected service. Monique also has not heard from her and is perplexed and worried. Where is Yolanda?

# Chapter 18

# DANNY O AND MONIQUE

I FINISHED MY ADMINISTRATIVE duties for the day at
4:30 and lay down on my bunk to kill the last hour of my
9x6 tour with the Mets game on tv.

"Cap, you've got an outside call," the house watchman's voice
blared over the intercom.

"Okay, thanks," I shouted back.

"Hello, is this Gene?" a female voice whispered.

"Yeah, Gene speaking. Who's this?"

"Monique . . . I've got some interesting information for you.
Can you stop by?"

"Sure. This evening after work good for you?"

"That'll work. See you then."

I was surprised to hear from her and intrigued by her message.
I hustled right over there as soon as my shift ended.

"You've got to promise me you won't tell anyone where you

got this," she opened, excitement and fear in her voice.

"You've got it. What's this about?"

"Arson. The arsonist. Let me fix us some drinks and I'll tell you about it."

I waited impatiently during the few minutes it took her to bring drinks and get settled across from me.

"Danny O was here last night. I had to let him in . . . I'm part of his compensation for doing Wainwright's dirty work. I think I'm the only women in his life, and he likes to talk to me, use me for a sounding board, like we're an item or something."

I nodded, encouraging her to go on.

"So after his usual blow job — which is easier for me, cause I can't stand to look at his evil face or smell his garlic breath — we're still in bed, he lights cigarettes for us, and he starts confiding in me. Seems he's still upset with your meeting yesterday with Dave. I listen, making sympathetic sounds, and we drift into other talk. Then he tells me about a job he's got for tonight.

"For his usual $1,000, he's supposed to set a fire in a proposed demolition site. The building's already scaffolded and scheduled for demolition next week.

"He's relaxed, goes into a lot of detail, like that the owners and construction workers for the demo company all get an extra ten percent hazard pay for buildings damaged by fire. Either the owner or their employees set the fire themselves or contract with a pro like Danny to do the job. Most of the vacant abandoned buildings are owned by the city now, by default, and the City picks up the tab.

"Danny says he likes jobs like this because they're low priority for fire investigation . . . the fires don't have to be big, and this cuts down the possibilities of injuries or deaths that would give them high priority.

"Danny doesn't drive so he takes public transportation to the location. He doesn't like cabs because they could leave a trail.

"So he tells me that today he's going to stop at a hardware store on 86th and buy a gallon of kerosene or paint thinner and put it in his shopping bag with a week's worth of newspapers. This plus a match is all the equipment he needs. Like he's bragging about how good he is."

"Did he tell you the address of the building?" I ask.

"No, but he did say he'd catch the downtown bus to 34th Street, transfer to the crosstown bus to 10th Avenue, then catch dinner at his favorite restaurant, Guido's Spaghetti Factory on 38th Street . . . said it was just a couple of blocks from the demo building."

"Okay. How's he going to get inside the building?"

"He said his clients usually leave a panel of plywood wall loose for him. That's when the crazy talk started. He starts laying it out for me step by step!"

"Like what, the job?"

"More! First he tells me about the Chianti he'll drink with dinner, how he'll tip the waiter and piano player before strolling down to 36th Street; how he'll check out the area even though only a few people still live on the block. How he'll pick a spot near a rear stairway and douse it with his accelerant and place the newspapers with some loose wood on top. He'll put the kerosene or whatever back in his bag before starting the fire. The he'll head for . . ."

"Okay Monique, I've got the picture. After dark, right?"

"Yeah."

"Can I use your phone?"

"Of course."

I call the fire house and get Gerry Guilfoyle. "Gerry, this is

Gene. Can you do me a favor and look up the Fire Marshall's office phone number? I'll fill you in when I see you."

I make the call and get, "Fire Marshall Roebline here."

Surprised to hear the voice, of a former E218 fireman, I reply, "Bill, this is Captain Gene, from the old days. I need a favor."

"Anything for you, Cap."

"I just got a tip that there's going to be an arson job on a demo site tonight on 36th Street just west of 10th Avenue. What do you recommend?"

"You know our manpower shortages, Gene. We've only got two teams working in the whole city, but if it's a slow night, we can do a surveillance. You know how crazy things can get. I'll notify the nearby firehouse and the local precinct, give them a heads up. Did you get a time frame on this?"

"Yeah. Probably between ten and midnight." I gave him a description of the perp.

"Where can I reach you?"

"I'm heading to Long Beach tonight and working days tomorrow." I give him both numbers.

At 1:00 a.m. Bill Roebling calls. "I know it's late, Cap, but thought you were anxious to know the outcome of tonight. It was Murphy's Law . . . everything went wrong. We had a stakeout until 10:00 p.m. when we were called to another high priority job. When that was finished we went to the 38th Street firehouse to see if anything'd happened.

"The firehouse's regular companies had been called downtown to the same job we went to. Don't know if you've seen it on the news, but there's a huge fire on an abandoned pier — still out of control. The Company that relocated to the 38th Street firehouse went to the 36th Street fire, knowing nothing about the circumstances. I'd contacted the local precinct and that was another disaster. They'd had a spot surveillance on the place; wouldn't sit on it but did respond to the fire, but there was nothing to report. The cops went off duty at midnight. I'll follow up ASAP to see if they have any information. It doesn't look good."

I thanked him for his effort. Some things just don't work out.

The next day I met Monique for coffee after work and told her what had happened.

"Monique, we need to know what Danny has to say about last evening. Don't push for information, let him come to you."

Two days later, Roebling calls with his follow up. He finally contacted the responding police radio unit. They had a periodic surveillance on the building but were out on another call when the fire came in. They picked it up on the air and arrived just as the fire department unit had gone to work. They questioned a civilian there who was slightly injured at the scene. His story was that he'd been coming from Guido's and saw the fire; hurried to get to an alarm box and fell near the scene, tripping over a cracked sidewalk. The two cops took him to Guido's to check out his story and the waiter confirmed that he'd just left there."

"Did you get a description?"

"Yeah. Cop said he was short, maybe five-five, dark skinned, dressed conservatively. No jewelry."

"Anything else?"

"Yeah. His English was pretty good; no accent."

"That was our arsonist, Bill. I was told by my informant that he planned to eat at Guido's before doing the job."

"Shit. Okay, Gene, I'll relay that to the precinct and see if they still have his name."

A few days later Roebling called to tell me that one of the cops did have the guy's name written down in his memo book, but it turned out to be false.

No sooner had I hung up than Monique called to tell me that Danny O seemed nervous, paranoid, hadn't wanted to talk about the other night beyond saying that everything had gone wrong. Murphy's Law prevailed.

# Chapter 19

# 30,000 ALARM RESPONSES WITHOUT AN ACCIDENT

ENGINE 218, MY first assignment in Bushwick, Brooklyn, had a plaque on the wall indicating 30,000 responses to alarms *without an accident.* In 1976 just before I was promoted to Captain, E 218 was slated to get a new engine pumper. The new engine was delivered from the Department of Repairs and Transportation where all new pumpers are tested.

On arrival at our firehouse the R&T unit saw our citation on the wall. They looked at our old beat-up pumper, saying it looked like one of General Patton's tanks used in the last major German offense in World War II. Looking again at the citation they asked, "Are you guys kidding?" With a straight face I confirmed that there were no reported accidents, adding that the streets were filled with potholes and though you could see most of our painted self-made repairs, that was our story! Despite all this, the next Engine Company that got our old pumper reported that it was in very good mechanical condition and, despite its bumps and bruises, they were very happy with it.

It's true there were no reported accidents, which was not to say there weren't accidents; we made repairs ourselves and sometimes even paid for the other involved vehicle repairs. We were willing to cover a few costs to obtain that 30,000-runs-without-an-accident citation which was truly a remarkable achievement for the tumultuous times we were in.

One particular accident comes to mind very vividly. On a response to an All-Hands fire, we had sideswiped a parked car while turning a corner. We looked, saw no occupant and continued to the fire. When operations were completed we went back to the scene. The car was no longer there! We returned to quarters, cleaned up and started to prepare our late evening meal. Two New York City policemen, John and Ed (who often ate evening meals with us) entered quarters with two females who had reported an accident with our apparatus. We acknowledged it was us and, thinking of our ongoing accident-free record, we offered to pay for the repairs at our neighborhood auto repair shop, which also handled our private car repairs. Since there were no injuries they agreed and we arranged for the repairs.

During these negotiations, John and Ed removed their caps and placed them over their chest shields, not wanting to be privy to this deal. As it later turned out, when the woman who owned the car went to our mechanic she had second thoughts on the arrangement and said she was thinking of getting a lawyer and suing.

The mechanic talked to her for a while and later told us he had said, "Are you for real, Lady? You're on welfare and any money received you are not entitled to as it goes back to the city." God somehow protects firemen, and all turned out well. The meal that night cost each man $43.00, which paid for the cost of the woman's repairs.

This was not the only unofficial incident, but in those days of fierce company pride, that 30,000 response award was very important. My first Captain wanted his 10,000 response award so badly that he told all our members to call him at home about any accidents and that he'd pay for all damages. Though 10,000 was large in those days, it was well below the amount of our present number of responses.

Another accident incident happened once when we were returning from a false alarm. Some streets in Brooklyn were extremely narrow, particularly for taking corners with a fire engine. This time we hit a car on the turn. We stopped and the owner appeared.

"Man, you hit my car and who's gonna pay for it?" he demanded.

As I dismounted, thinking about what kind of offer to make, fireman Marty Keane, left his rear seat and confronted the owner, saying, "Do you believe in God, Man?"

Thrown off his objective, the owner answered , "Yeah. Sure. I do."

Marty went on: "Did you know we're doing God's work and you are *not right* in what you've asked."

Slightly perplexed, the guy tells us that he's sorry and to forget about it and have a good day. Though his car was slightly banged up in other spots I still made him an small offer. "No man, you guys are doing a good job," he says and went on his way. I know Somebody Up There likes us!

# Chapter 20

# THE PERFECT FIRE

WITH TWENTY YEARS in the fire service, I retain the feelings I had when I first came in. I never imagined I'd feel about *anything* the way I do about the Fire Department, and I'm not alone in this. My feelings towards brother fireman — the camaraderie, the closeness of the fire-fighting family, the stripping to the bone of all facades during fires — reveals the inner truth of every fireman. All of us get a clear concise picture of what we are. We rarely criticized each other's performance, as long as we were giving our best shot. The highest compliment any of us receive is to be called a good fireman. We didn't *need* criticism from others, because we continually critiqued our own performances, always asking ourselves, "Can I do better next time?" The feeling of wonder when you walk away from a good job is all the incentive we need to improve. A perfect job, like a perfect no hitter, may come once in a lifetime. It's like throwing a perfect game in baseball: the pitcher has to have top performance from himself plus a team behind him that is flawless. Twenty seven straight outs, no walks, no errors, good calls by the umpires, good plays and balls just barely going foul are rare. I remember such a perfect job at a fire I was involved in at E218 in Brooklyn.

We had been called to an ADV fire (abandoned derelict vehicle) on Evergreen, near Bushwick, at 3:30 a.m. We responded, extinguishing the fire with our truck's booster hose. After operations we went back in service on the department radio. We were just about in our seats when we get a call to respond to a fire on Bushwick a few blocks away.

We turned the corner onto Bushwick and saw a man with his head out a building window, smoke bellowing out around him. I transmitted a 10-75 signal for a working fire, reporting that the building was attached to a similar building "old law" type tenement (built before 1929), that allows a fireman to access the roof from the adjoining building. The burning building was four stories high with a man hanging out the top floor window. I asked the dispatcher to send a full First Alarm assignment comprised of three engines and two trucks.

We pulled in front of the building and spotted a hydrant only a few doors away, a comparatively short stretch. With a six-man crew assigned to busier companies, I always assigned one man to open the roof if needed, in case the incoming ladder companies were at other work or delayed. Jim Park was assigned to enter the adjoining building and proceed to the roof of the fire building to open the bulkhead door. He was to then rejoin the company at the point of operation because he had no way of communicating with us, which could have put him in a dangerous position.

Meanwhile I entered the first floor hallway. The smoke and visibility were down to two feet from the floor. The men were hooking up and starting the stretch, a good fast stretch. The mandatory use of masks by all was soon to come, but for now our engine company standard operation was for the company to stretch to the point of the fire and then the last two men on the line would drop back for their masks. If we could make it without masks we would; if not, the masked men would relieve the men up front. The reason for this flexible operation was that wood frame structures burned like tinder boxes, and fires traveled so fast that the limited visibility masks could be a problem. No one could sense or feel all the possible dangerous situations we could be in when wearing gloves and a mask; I usually took off one glove so I could feel the intensity of the surrounding heat.

When I entered the hall I assumed the fire was somewhere in an above apartment. As I approached the stairway I hear a cry for help from the second floor. Staying low to the floor, I headed for the sound and encountered a woman cringing near the floor. I started to take her down the stairs but she pulled away from me. I heard Jimmy Hoffmier, my control man (who had to find me so he'd know where to bring the hose line) calling me, "Where are you, Lou?" (short for Lieutenant) He followed my response and the woman's cries. I suddenly realized why she was pulling away when I heard another cry behind her. It was her daughter whom we later learned was autistic.

Jimmy was now with me. I grabbed the child, he grabbed the mother and we half tumbled down the stairs. Descending, I felt an intense heat on my neck and realized it was coming from below the second floor. Jim Park had suddenly opened the roof door and visibility improved. We brought the two down to the street and handed them over to the Chief and his driver. The incoming units were now arriving.

I headed back, realizing that there was a fire in the cellar. The door was opened and intense heat and smoke rose from below. I yelled to Pace, the now masked nozzle man, that the fire was in the cellar. As I closed the cellar door he was right behind me, the hose charged with water and ready to go. The roof was opened and the source of the heat and smoke had been cut off.

Miraculously, the heat and smoke suddenly lifted from the interior hall, from the first floor to the roof. Now the arriving truck companies were making a search throughout the building. We kept the hose line there to protect the hallway. The nozzle man, Buddy Pace, who had gone back for a mask, cracked the cellar door to take a look and exclaimed through his mask, "Lou, I think we can make it down." He opened the nozzle into the crack and then opened the door fully, pushing the heat and smoke down the stairs as he descended.

Hoffmier had returned wearing his mask to back up Pace on the nozzle and they saw the Red Devil in its lair in the rear of the cellar. With one long thrust of the heavy hose stream, he pierced it's heart and extinguished all flames — a remarkable job from Fireman Pace, one of the most experienced, knowledgeable fire fighters and an informal leader of the men whom I relied on.

Later I learned that while he was waiting for water and the hall was clearing of smoke, Pace had raced up to the fourth floor and brought down the man who'd been hanging out of the window.

When it was over, the Chief realized what a great job we had done. No one was hurt, property damage was limited to some old stacked newspapers and old stored furniture in the basement.

Most of the perilous actions had taken place before any other units had arrived.

The Chief of the 35th battalion lets us know he felt we'd done a great job and he intended to write us up. Engine Company 218 receives a Unit Citation and three Class A medals, for Firemen Hoffmier, Fireman Pace and myself. It was a job that I'll never forget. Engine companies whose responsibility is mainly to put out fires are not expected to rescue and vent: those are things the Ladder companies usually do and, as a result, they get most of the citations and medals. For us to get three A's and a Unit Citation was very unusual for an Engine Company. We all felt exhilarated, as if we had pitched a perfect game.

# Chapter 21

# ELIZABETH CALLS

E LIZABETH CALLED MY house in Long Beach, leaving a call-back message with Dick. The number appeared to be for her home phone in Woodside, Queens.

"Gene. Thanks for returning my call. Can I meet you somewhere? I have some information I'd like to discuss with you."

I know Woodside very well, so I suggested we meet at Donovan's, a local restaurant and bar with good hearty food and a friendly crowd.

"Oh, sure. I know Donovan's. It's not far from where I live."

We shoot for nine o'clock that evening.

\* \* \*

When she walks into Donovan's bar I am struck by her deep green eyes, pale skin and beautifully sculptured face. Her long brown hair is pulled to the side in a tortoise shell clip at the nape of her neck. Late thirties I guess. She takes off her trench coat while scanning the busy bar. Conservatively dressed. I wave, she spots me and smiles, navigating through the thick smoky standing-room-only crowd .

"Busy bar," she says loudly, looking around. Somebody accidentally bumps her. "Sorry," he says. Elizabeth smiles and stands a bit closer to me. Her expression suddenly changes. "Uh-oh. Maybe this place is a little *too* popular," she says, sending a perfunctory smile and wave to an older woman at the end of the bar.

Melanie Safka's pop hit "Brand New Key" is playing on the jukebox. "I love this song," Elizabeth says as she leans in closer to listen:

*I rode my bicycle past your window last night*
*I roller skated to your door at daylight*
*It almost seems that you're avoiding me*
*I'm ok alone but you've got something I need*

"My Dad used to hang out here. Every now and again I'd have to pick him up . . . a little too over-served, if you know what I mean," she says rolling her eyes. I laugh and she steps in even closer.

"I'm from a long line of civil servants and very proud to be part of that heritage. It's part of the reason I became an FBI agent," she explains.

"My Dad's dad helped organize the first NYPD back in 1898. Dad's a retired cop, almost twenty five years on the job. My uncle's also a cop. It's in the blood, I guess.

I'm intrigued, less by her impressive lineage than by the sincerity I can see in her pretty green eyes. She likes me, I can tell, but she's hiding something. I wonder and smile back at her. "Well then, it must be genetic," is all I can say.

*I ride my bike, I roller skate, don't drive no car*
*Don't go too fast, but I go pretty far*
*For somebody who don't drive I've been all around the world*
*Some people say I've done all right for a girl*

I lean in to Elizabeth's ear and ask if she'd like to have dinner. She nods yes with a big smile. I settle with the bartender and we follow the hostess to a table in the back dining room. At last, quiet.

Over drinks, we exchange glimpses into our lives. Elizabeth talked about her mother's early death, her decision to become a nun and the deep disappointment it caused her father; how he adjusted to it and moved near her convent in Pennsylvania when he retired, even becoming involved with parents of other girls in her Order . "Eventually," Elizabeth confessed, "I figured out that I'd only wanted to become a nun because my mother wanted that for me. I realized I really didn't have the vocation, so I left. So here I am. I love the FBI. I'm happy."

Over a second cocktail, Elizabeth moved the conversation toward my personal life. I told her how my father had deserted us during World War II, how we held things together on a shoe string until my brother got out of the service and things got easier.

"Must have been tough," Elizabeth says, real concern in her eyes. "Tell me about it."

I wet my whistle and begin:

"In 1946, at not quite 16, I had to quit high school and go to work. My best friend, Hank, had a job as an office boy and he told me there was another opening. The take home pay was $26 a week. $20 of that went to my mother. I was the oldest at home, with a twin brother and sister just seven years old, and a nine year old brother and a sister who was twelve.

"Theresa, my mother, had a lot of spirit and the courage of a lioness protecting her cubs. In spite of the harshness and disappointments, she often said later that this was one of the happiest times of her life because we were all together, working to keep the family intact. We had to move from our nice apartment in Richmond Hill, Queens, when the building was sold and the new owner wanted our apartment for himself. He made a deal with my mother: he paid all our moving expenses and two month's rent at our new place, which was in the new Quonset Hut Apartment Complex in Brooklyn. The Quonset Hut had been built as emergency housing for returning GIs. This, like many developments in the City, was built with army surplus material. Because my older brother Al was in the service, we were eligible for an apartment.

"Somehow we pulled through with my salary and baby sitting jobs my sister and I had in the Complex. With help from our church and from "home relief," a shameful position to be in at that time, we managed to make it.

"After a couple of years I worked my way into a bookkeeper position — a turning point in my life. On my morning commute by bus and subway to Manhattan, I'd often ride with Ed Suffel, a vet who was a Court Officer in the City. He'd returned with a Belgium war bride and her six year old daughter whom he'd adopted. I often babysat for them on a Friday or Saturday night, and Ed soon became a father figure for me. One day on the way to work, he tells me about a Civil Service Test for the Police Department, one that didn't require a high school diploma . . . you just needed to be nineteen, which I was. If you passed all the requirements you could get appointed when you turned twenty one. Ed told me how to get the application, then he helped me fill it out and set up a study schedule for me. Each week he'd give me assignments to read — penal law, civics, reading interpretation, etc., and the following week he'd test me. After a year of this intensive learning, I was ready for the test. I knocked it stiff and was appointed in the first class. "

"That's great, Gene, and you obviously earned it!"

"Yeah, I worked hard, but I've often wondered where I'd have been without Ed. My mentor and my lifelong friend."

"Yes, Ed was a lucky break for you, but you're still the one who did the work. What happened after that?"

"I was drafted into the Korean War, became a police officer, then a fireman after my military service. I married at twenty-nine for all the wrong reasons, had three kids and, after twenty years, decided to get out — to put an end to my unhappiness and unhealthy pastimes. I swallowed my guilt and got out, but made sure the family was taken care of."

We order a final round and I explain that the separation started a year ago, and that I'd seen a Fire Department psychologist to help me cope with the changes in my life. "Haven't had any heavy drinking episodes since then," I proudly announced.

Elizabeth nods, digesting my confession and asks if I have any pictures of my kids. She stares at them for a long while and finally says, "They're all three really good looking."

This evening is almost too nice to end. After diner I ask if I can walk her home.

"I enjoy walking and that sounds like a good idea," she agrees.

* * *

As we stroll, I remember answering calls in this area when I was a firemen here, over fifteen years ago. There's nostalgia for me in these tree-lined streets of connected houses in this very Irish, tightly knit neighborhood. We pass the softball field and I remember playing against the other fire houses, the hot dogs, hamburgers and barrels of beer we shared.

I am still blabbing when we arrived at Elizabeth's home, and she still seems interested. At the steps to her attached brick house she turns to me.

"I can't tell you how much I've enjoyed this evening," I say. "Would you like to do it again?"

She grasps my hand and gently kisses me on the lips. "I had a great time, Gene. I'd love to do it again."

She skips up the steps. I wait for her to open her door and go in. She looks back at me and waves. I wave back, feeling like a kid again. On my way back to Donovan's I replay her reaction over and over. I have a feeling that something very nice is happening.

Suddenly it occurred to me that she'd never told me about the information she had for me.

# Chapter 22

# DANNY O WITH DAVE

"HEY, GENE. IT'S MONIQUE. I had another little talk with Danny O and thought you'd be interested. When can you come by?"

I stroll over to Monique's as soon as my shift ends. She fixes us drinks, hers a virgin Bloody Mary, and we settle before she begins.

"So Danny O finally reaches Dave and finds out he's been away on business — as he would've known in his earlier calls if he'd been a little more patient and listened to the whole message. Danny tells Dave he needs to meet with him right away and suggests it be away from his office or Wainwright Hall. Dave says he'll meet him at The Victory Café, on 93rd and Third Avenue after office hours, at 6:00 p.m. Dave told me later he'd chosen a public place because he doesn't like being alone with trouble, and Danny O has been pretty nervous lately.

"They each arrive at The Victory Café about the same time. It's early and the place isn't busy yet. Dave chooses a table in the far corner. After ordering drinks, Danny leans across the table and lays into Dave. "Why the hell would you hire a *fire captain* as a consultant?!" he furiously demands to know. Dave looks at him as if he was crazy, so Danny tells Dave about me telling him about meeting the Captain twice. Danny says he repeated 'two times' and underscored it by shoving two fingers in Dave's face.

"Then Dave grabs Danny's wrist and glares at him. Getting the message, Danny calmed himself and explained to Dave that the fire captain could become aware of some of the arson jobs and some of the hiring of the supers through their connection to the 86th Street apartment house.

"Danny starts fuming again. He knew the building was loaded with drug operations plus various other illegal activities, some that Danny himself was involved in. He didn't want anyone with know-how and authority snooping around.

"What the fuck is going on, Dave?" Danny demanded. Dave just stared at him; it took a minute for him to digest the implications of what Danny was telling him.

Then, Danny said, Dave looked calmly at him and his flaring nostrils and explained how he knew nothing of the captain's background . . . that it had been a chance meeting, in response to a fire call at his penthouse, and how could he know of any connection with Monique? Dave told Danny he'd get to the bottom of this and see if there was anything to worry about. He wasn't comfortable with this new development either. Dave tossed a twenty on the table and left.

"A few minutes after Danny left my place, Dave called, sounding out how he's going to handle this. He wants to use a subtle approach, avoid any possible suspicions. He decides to confront you, Gene, and to do so on the first day of the trial job, but in an oblique manner so as to not create any accelerated interest in him.

"With his mind settled about that, Dave rambles about his involvement with Danny and his disgust at being bedfellows with him. He talked about his poor but honest youth on the West Side and of how sickened his father would be by his actions. Dave has always held his head high, particularly with his army record. He used to feel proud, but no more . . . he knew he'd made a mistake when he first laid eyes on that piece of shit.

"I'm not sure what's going down, Gene, but I'd watch out for both Dave and Danny if I were you."

"Gotcha. Thanks, Monique. I owe you."

# Chapter 23

# MONIQUE — A REKINDLE

TWO NIGHTS LATER. The evening of another lovely day, Monique approaches the firehouse and sees me standing near the entrance along with several other firemen. She gets the picture immediately. This is the hour when all the young women are returning from work downtown on the Lexington Avenue subway. It is definitely ogling time. I walk over to her, give her a hug for the benefit of the firemen, ask how she is and has she seen Yolanda, which she has not. We are both concerned about Yolanda's absence.

"I stopped by last night, " Monique says. "I was disappointed to miss you but not sorry I came. There was this young fireman standing by the open entrance. I said hi, giving my best smile to this strong, virile looking guy and I liked the way he said hi back. He was young, but I liked the way he made me feel; a feeling I haven't experienced for a long time. I told him I was a friend of yours and would like to see you. He said that 'the Captain' wasn't working that day but he'd find out when you'd be on your next tour. He checked with the officer on duty and said you'd be in today. I thanked him with another big smile and said I'd be back. I could tell he wasn't missing a single sway of my hips, or my red hair. It felt sooo good!"

With a happy sigh, she gets down to business. She reminds me how agitated Danny O got when she told him of her chance meeting with me in the Wainwright Hall lobby . . . how his agitation escalated when she told him about being on a triple date with Yolanda, her daughter, me and two other firemen, and that I had come to her apartment at Yolanda's request, to help move some furniture. She was astonished by his reaction because she knew what a dangerous man Danny O was. "I don't like it, Gene."

"I'm starting the job with Dave on Monday," I casually reply, "and I'll mention our chance meeting in Wainwright Hall and some other particulars to see what his thoughts are. I'll play dumb and simple — how I met Yolanda, dated a few times and that's the extent of it. What Yolanda had told me about Danny O and Wainwright Management is out of the equation."

Monique seems relieved, tells me how much she likes me and I reply the same. She leaves with a smile and her great body movements, not a single fireman missing anything. I'll have to invent a great story to make their tongues hang out. I tell them to assemble all members to shop for our meal.

The members have decided on a pork chop dinner with sauerkraut and mashed potatoes and, naturally, dessert. At Gristiedes all the members except for my chauffeur, Joe Moore, head into the store with their shopping list. I tell Joe I'm going to take a short walk and enjoy the beautiful evening. Actually I wanted to be alone to digest my meeting with Monique. I make a mental note that in this adventure I am going to be accompanied by my 38 caliber colt pistol with a barrel I had shortened to make it less noticeable.

Back at the firehouse I work on reports while the men prepare the meal. At 9:30 p.m. we sit down to fine dinner of pork chops baked with catsup and smothered with sautéed onions to mix with the mashed potatoes. I often wondered about opening a restaurant with food as good as this.

At 10:53 I'm in my office and the men are in the basement watching a baseball game on television. We get an alarm for an odor of smoke in a grocery store on 89th and Second Avenue. The manager of the large independent food store tells us he smells smoke in the basement and doesn't know where it's coming from. My ladder unit along with Chief McCarney of the 10th Battalion start looking for sources of the smoke. After checking all possibilities such as lights, electrical wiring, pipe and beam openings in walls, we come up with nothing. I tell my roof man and chauffeur to check the building next door; send my outside vent man and forcible entry team to check the floors above: still nothing. Joe Moore, my chauffeur, tells me the restaurant next door is closed and from a look into the front window, it appears normal. We check the building top to bottom and cannot come up with anything. We're there at least 45 minutes. Finally someone feels the ballast box of a florescent fixture. It feels hot and gives off a smell of smoke. The smoke in the basement seems to now be dissipated and we assume the heated ballast box was the cause. We take up and return to the firehouse.

At 1:30 a.m. we get an alarm for a fire at the same location.

It's a rekindle. We're going back to fight the real fire. In over 20 years in the job I had never had a rekindle but now I know the feeling and it isn't good. It casts aspersions on our knowledge and professionalism.

When we arrive occupants are on the fire escape of the apartment above the store. There is an extremely heavy smoke condition but as yet no visible fire. The engine stretches a line into the building and waits for the ladder truck to find the fire. We evacuate the whole building and start looking. With masks on it's very difficult to see, adding to the problem. Some truckies wear what they call cheaters, which are a scuba diving mouth piece with no face masks Cheaters are not allowed officially but men use them as it effectively gives them visibility. However, the damage to your eyes causes severe conjunctivitis in later years.

Finally on the second floor on the wall adjoining the restaurant we feel extreme heat. My men probe the wall and suddenly fire flashes out. I call on my handi talkie to the engine company to bring the line to the second floor: We have found the fire. We continue to tear down the wall. A lot of fire is showing, which the engine hose line quickly extinguishes. The hose is inserted into the wall and operated up and down to extinguish the fire inside the wall. Chief McCartney has already dispatched units to the floor above to open all walls adjoining the next door building up to the roof. Another truck and engine are dispatched to the restaurant where there is a little smoke but no fire. After the restaurant has cleared of smoke, they check the other side of the adjoining wall. They check a fireplace, find it very hot to the touch, and knock out the fireplace ceramic flue walls, where the origin of the fire is found. While the fireplace had been lit for dinning pleasure earlier in the evening, fire had extended behind the fireplace flue wall and lit the wood beams behind the fireplace. It must have smoldered a long time and finally broken out in flames.

We know what our mistake was. The owner of the restaurant should have been called on the initial call. He was there now. Either that or we should have used forcible entry for access to the restaurant. We'd made a mistake and we all knew it, a really bad feeling. We hadn't done our job well and now there has been loss of property to fire and smoke damage. Fortunately there were no injuries or deaths and not too much damage to the occupant's apartments. Still no excuse; we all felt like shit!

# Chapter 24

# STARTING THE JOB

I ARRIVED EARLY AT Wainwright Hall. Jim Spencer had already started his day. He has other buildings to look at and will be gone most of the day so he gives me a key to his office and tells me to make myself at home. He's already put on a pot of coffee and after he leaves I have coffee and plan my approach to the building evaluation. I'd brought my "standard form of orders," which we use for our inspection in the fire department. The list covers building and electrical department codes as well as state laws pertaining to residence buildings.

I lock the office door and take the elevator to the top floor, the fortieth. Access to the roof is in compliance: no locks. I open the slide bolt and enter the roof. I note a blocked drain with a slight buildup of water; they have to be checked on a periodic basis to prevent water damage to the roof. Descending the stairs I note that all the fire evacuation signs are posted and see that Jim

Spencer is doing a good job. I head down, checking various self closing door devices, making note of the few that were not closing completely, which is important for limiting the spread of fire. I see that the halls on each of the floors are way too long. I definitely will recommend the addition of new self closing doors to be installed half-way down each hallway. This will cut down the chance of fire, smoke and heat spreading the whole length of the hall.

On each of the floors I check the standpipes to see that the hoses are intact and that no dry rot is in evidence. At the twentieth floor I check the pumping station, which is enclosed in a small room, to see that the monthly inspections have been done and recorded. This pumping station supplies the water to the standpipe outlets on each of the above floors. I continue my walk down all the way to the basement and check the other pumping station that delivers water to the standpipes and sprinklers of the first twenty floors. I note that there are also adequate signs in this pumping station on how to shut down the system in case of emergency. At one building on Park Avenue, my men and I waded into hip high water caused by a busted water pipe. There were no schematic signs posted in their rather large pumping station on how to shut down the system, which could result in a lot of water damage to the basement because we just close all the valves until we happen onto the right one. I complete my inspection about 1:30, leave a note that I'm going to lunch and will be back at 2:30.

On my return I typed up my inspection report and recommendations. I finished an hour or so later and was lighting a cigarette when Jim Spencer returned. I told him that his posted fire evacuation plans were excellent and easy to follow. He seems pleased. As we talk, Dave Maier walks in and asks how things had gone. Jim says he is done for the day, has to catch a Long Island train, and departs. I show Dave the results of my cursory inspection and recommendations and he tells me he'll look at the report in his office tomorrow and also will I look at Curzon House next Monday, Oct. 7th. I tell him I will and he says he's had a very trying day, knows a good pub down the block and would I like to have a drink with him. I tell him that sounds good and we head for a place called Winters Café on 92nd Street. I'd been there before.

He picks a nice table and we order. After checking the bevy of attractive business women, Dave notes that this is a great place to meet good looking and interesting ladies. We seem to be on the same wavelength and our conversation has a good and easy flow. He tells me that he'd been looking at my resume earlier and asks where I served in the Army.

"Went to Korea in 1952 and was awarded the Combat Infantry Badge (C.I.B.) with two stars for service at Pork Chop Hill and Old Baldy."

His face lights up with interest and he tells me about his serving in World War II with Patton's Tank Corps. and how early in 1953 he was activated for Korea when manpower was running low and promoted to Major serving for the last three months of the "Police Action." Despite what I know and dislike about him, our army backgrounds create a certain connection. Dave mentions how much he'd enjoyed and been proud of his service to his country. "My only wish was that I could have the same feelings of satisfaction in civilian life but being in business, where it's dog eat dog, you don't get such feelings."

In an off-handed way he brings up my meeting in the lobby

with Monique, and his surprise that we knew each other since we seemed to come from very different worlds. Very matter of factly, I tell him that I had met her through a common friend, Yolanda, whom I had met when she came to the firehouse with a complaint. "Yolanda was very attractive. I asked her out a few times — hey, we even went on a triple date with Yolanda's grown daughter and Monique. Yolanda had kind of hinted to me about Monique's occupation but her date had found her to be a very nice person.'" I briefly explained that our chance meeting in the lobby was not the first meeting and I told him of the furniture moving. "What I love about New York is being able to meet people of all walks of life."

I casually look for a reaction and see none. We have two more drinks and he tells me he has enjoyed our talk together, particularly about our army experiences, and he'll probably see me next Monday.

# Chapter 25

# THE CURZON HOUSE INSPECTION

THE FOLLOWING MONDAY I head for the Curzon House on 70th Street for a familiarization and inspection of the building. Dave had said to contact Bill Henry, who manages both Wainwright Hall and The Curzon House. At 9:00 a.m. I arrive and I'm directed to Bill's office by a immaculately uniformed doorman, whom I had seen before at Carlows East.

Like Jim Spencer, Bill Henry is friendly and invites me to make myself at home. Over coffee he tells me he'll help in any building familiarization and gives me a complete set of keys for access to storage rooms in the basement, pump houses, outside roof doors and various other locked areas. He says he will take me to the roof and on the way will answer any questions I might have about the building which I find, like the other building, to be extremely well taken care of and well managed, which is not an easy job.

Working from the roof down I find only a few minor violations. A basement storage area that, due to a large amount of tenant property, poses a possible access problem in case of fire or an emergency. The sprinkler system in various required locations cuts down any major problems with a fire. I finish the inspection, do a report in Bill's office and ask if he can give it to Dave. About 3:30 I head up to Carlows East. I note to myself that even with a third building property there wouldn't be enough need to create a full time job for me since there is an excellent Fire Safety Director and Buildings Manager on board. A part-time consultant's job of some order might be the direction to go.

I find a quiet small crowd at Carlows with my favorite bartender and owner, Jim Hyland, who loves firemen. He and his partner had bought this bar and building, which also contained six apartments, for a song a few years before and with the real estate market on the upper East Side going out of sight, they were sitting on a gold mine. It couldn't happen to two nicer guys. After our run through of sports, politics, our city softball championship, he gets a little busy and I enjoy the few beers wondering where and what I'm to do next in this Wainwright situation.. My disgust for Dave has somewhat diminished because of what I'd found out about him that I like. Danny O is another story. Though I've never met him I know he is just a criminal thug well connected to the underworld crime families and very dangerous and not to be underestimated. I tell Jim I have a couple of important phone calls to make and ask to use his office for privacy. No sooner said, he flips the office keys to me.

I call Elizabeth at home but as expected she is not there so I leave a message to call me tonight in Long Beach. I call Monique at home with better results; she is her usual excited self. I tell her that I have a few things I'd like to discuss. "I'm free now if that's okay," and we agree to meet in half an hour at a place between here and her apartment..

I walk the three blocks to Rathbones, order a drink and wait for Monique. In a few minutes she bounces through the door. As I order her a drink she stops me, saying she's in AA and a Virgin Bloody Mary would be perfect.

I thank her again for coming to the firehouse with her concern over Danny O and ask if she could help me out with some information about him. "It'll be strictly confidential," I assure her, in case she has any apprehension.

"Don't worry about it. He's just a creep," she says.

I launch right in.

"What's his real name, where does he live and does he have a telephone?" She has all three answers: Dante Occhionero, living at the Housing Projects on 94th and First Avenue and his telephone number is also given. Monique is one smart cookie. She asks no further questions and tells me she trusts me completely.

Monique is very easy to talk to. I tell her a few things about me, my job, my separated family, my children. We talk about Yolanda and she volunteers that she hasn't heard a word from her and is very worried.

Suddenly, very serious, she tells me her current way of making a living is growing old and stale. " But how would a person like me ever have a normal life?" A tear forms in the corner of her eye. "I don't know what a normal life is."

She tells me how she'd kicked her alcohol/drug abuse and is in an AA program that's made her feel much better about herself.

"Meeting a nice normal guy like Jerry, makes me realize what a negative life I lead."

She tells me she has built up a good nest egg but doesn't know how to go about changing her life.

"Hey, start looking at the positive things in your life! You're clean from alcohol and drugs and financially secure. Things could be a lot worse! You've got to start thinking how you can break away from the present, start making a change.

"Tell you what, next week when I'm at Wainwright Hall we should sit down together and talk about possible solutions."

She breaks out a mirror, sees her streaked mascara and, laughs. "I feel a little better after talking with you, Gene, and I'll think about what you've said.

I feel a pang of sympathy for Monique as I walk back to the firehouse. She is a really nice person and maybe I can help. "She who rides the tiger cannot dismount." Well, maybe!

# Chapter 26

# RESPITE AT LONG BEACH

AFTER LEAVING MONIQUE I head back to Long
Beach for two more days off and a much needed rest. I
will work Friday and Saturday day tours and then start
a two week vacation which will include spending some time with
my daughters, Ann and Mary. My daughter Ann is interested in
fashion and just started her first semester at the Fashion Institute
of Technology (F.I.T.) in September and has an extended weekend coming up because of the Columbus Day holiday. I can't
wait to talk with her. She is looking for some part-time work and
an apartment in Manhattan to share with two other students. I'm
going to ask Don Lenahan for any part time positions he might
have for Monique at his furniture showroom and warehouse at
72nd and Second Avenue. Many of my men were given good furniture deals from Don because he grew up with Jim Graham, a
fireman assigned to our company.

My first stop in Long Beach is at The Saloon, where I know I'll run into a group of fireman who hang out there. My car has never been able to drive past The Saloon without stopping; it makes an uncontrollable thrust to the curb. After drinking a few beers at the bar and catching up with the latest news from my friends, I'll sit down to their specialty, a seafood dinner with lobster bits, scallops, shrimp, calamari and clams over spaghetti with marinara sauce, and a bottle of Chianti to complete the pleasure. My roommate Dick Keenan, happens by and decides to join me. We stay later than expected.

When we get home I see I have a message on my machine from Elizabeth. Though it's a little late, I decide to call her.

"I'm glad you called. I have some news for you," she says. In the process of their FBI investigation of Wainwright Management, her boss, Bill Wilson, decided Yolanda might be a source of information. Knowing that Yolanda has worked for the C.I.A., they thought that would be a good place to start to locate her.

"Bingo! They found out she's been back working for the C.I.A. for a month and is right now in Fort Chaffee, Arkansas interviewing and interrogating some of the Boat People that Castro recently freed from Cuba."

Her C.I.A. background in Cuba and her fluent Spanish made her very valuable. Elizabeth's team is considering contacting Yolanda for an interview because of the information I had provided.

"Would you mind coming to headquarters to touch bases on some aspects of our investigation?" Elizabeth asks.

"No problem. Would you like to go to dinner?" I was elated when she said sure. I suggested Sans Cullotte on 57th Street and Second Avenue "They have great food and a neat piano player who does a spectacular singing imitation of Elvis Presley," I tell her. "My two favorites are *Moody Blues* and *Danny Boy*. Close your eyes and it's as if Elvis is there. Saturday is my last tour before a vacation . . . a dinner with you would be a nice start."

"Sounds good. I'm off Saturday and you'll be working days. How about if I just take the subway from Woodside to Manhattan?"

She's a real blue collar gal! "Seven o'clock okay?" She agrees and says she'll meet me at the restaurant.

The next morning I'm looking forward to a couple of uneventful days relaxing in Long Beach. Nothing is nicer than walking the flat beach at low tide in the fall, catching beautiful sunsets and much needed rest and renewal on my 'Contemplation Rock.' But one of the first things I'll do this morning is call Monique to tell her about Yolanda. She's ecstatic that Yolanda is safe.

"I've thought about our discussion at Rathbones the other day and I have a few life changing ideas," she says laughingly. She agrees to meet me for lunch on Monday, when I'll be at Wainwright Hall.

"I'll call for you at your apartment around noon."

# Chapter 27

# MY BIGGEST FIRE

MY LONG BEACH days off and my upcoming vacation make working Friday and Saturday very enjoyable. I'm full of anticipation, like a kid waiting for summer break. I'll spend both days making sure all administrative duties are complete because I don't want to leave a mess for the captain covering my vacation.

About ten o'clock the department city-wide radio announces a factory fire in downtown New York. This city-wide network is activated to reach all companies on the job, rather than the usual selectives that go out to only operating companies within our alarm assisgnment area. Within an hour eight full first-alarm assignments have been transmitted and the factory fire had extended to three other adjoining buildings.

Tower Ladder 13 is not on any assignment card for that area but we get a call over the department phone that all factories have been vacated and streams from tower ladders were needed to control this huge fire.

Heading from 85th Street to downtown New York's Vecsey Street is an adventure in itself with the huge amount of traffic in midtown Manhattan. We assumed that traffic on East River Drive and Westside Highway would be backed up because of the fire and taking local streets would be best. Eventually, at least twenty minutes later, we arrive at the scene and report to the officer in command.

The fire boats are drafting water from the Hudson River to one pumper three blocks away and that pumper was relaying the water to another pumper closer to the buildings involved, now counting five. All the pumpers being supplied water are in turn supplying tower ladders' streams to stop this fire from spreading. It has now reached ten full alarms.

The chief in charge plants our tower ladder in front of a nine story factory fully involved inside its walls with fire. We position our apparatus and are waiting for an engine company to supply us with water when Ed Duignan, a fairly new fireman comes over and exclaims, "Cap, I don't like the way the front wall of the building looks, it seems to be pulling away from the wall!" I look and sure enough he's right. The chief is standing near the apparatus and I inform him of this observation. He quickly orders our tower ladder moved.

The building is approximately ninety feet high. The fall zone of a collapsed building is about one-third of the building's height, thrity feet. Our apparatus sat twenty feet away from the building. Our relief chauffeur quickly backs into a parking lot and within three minutes the whole front wall comes crashing into the street with a thunderous sound which in itself causes men to run. After

the dust and stone clear, the chief runs over to congratulate me.
I bring over Firefighter Duignan and tell the chief that he was the
one who noticed the first indication of the collapse. The chief
says he'll send a letter through channels of commendation for FF.
Duignan, who beams with the recognition.

At five o'clock, on our way back to quarters, the full impact
of the possibilities hit me. I think of a good rope with its inter-
twined strands that determine the tensile strength of the rope,
each strand with significant importance. It is like our company
with its tensile strength and how good it is and I let them know
it. We'll drink a few happy beers when we get off work and head
to Carlow's.

# Chapter 28

# SECOND DATE WITH ELIZABETH

D RIVING INTO THE city from Long Beach on Saturday, without the weekday traffic is always a pleasure. I bring a change of clothes for tonight's date with Elizabeth. At the firehouse I catch up with all the unfinished paperwork I wanted to do yesterday. In the officer's bathroom I shower and dress, excited about our date. I stop at Carlows and buy the off-going tour a drink for my vacation, and then head to the restaurant.

I arrive a little early and decide to wait outside and enjoy the flavor of this part of the City, still considered uptown. With the shops and crowds on the streets it's stimulating. I see Elizabeth walking down from 59th Street and can't help but admire her. She greets me with a soft tender kiss.

Sans Culotte is as expected. The food is good, the cocktails well presented and the piano player is entertaining and talented.

I request my two Elvis favorites, *Moody Blues* and *Danny Boy*. I tell Elizabeth that I particularly love the range Elvis hit in *Danny Boy* as he ends the song.

After dinner and between dances I mention that I have some added information on Danny O. I briefly tell her of my source, Monique, and her setup as a result of Dave Maier helping her through some tough times. Also that Danny O is one of her distasteful commitments to Dave. I give Elizabeth his full name, address and telephone number.

"This is the one area we haven't been able to make any headway in. We've checked all our sources and haven't been able to get a make on Danny O," she says. "We've tapped Dave's phones, even had some surveillance on him but came up with nothing."

"One of his hangouts and job contacts is through the super at the building on 86th and Third Avenue," I tell her.

"We know that building," she relays. "There's been other underworld activity there, particularly relating to drugs, but nothing on Danny O. We're going to send an agent — maybe me — to interview Yolanda in Fort Chaffee, Kansas.

"My boss has authorized me to give you this information otherwise I couldn't tell you, and I know he'll be pleased with yours."

I kid her about how hard it is to get information from the FBI and how little they give out, regardless of how it retards other agencies' activities and enforcement.

She smiles and tells me that her dad, a former New York City Policeman, often mentions the one-way attitude of the FBI. "But Bill is different, Gene. He doesn't follow that mode."

We dance and talk further and each time we dance our bodies are a little closer together. At about 9:30, I get the check and tell her I'd like to drive her home with maybe a short stop for a nightcap at the Merry Go Round, a bar near her house.

She'd never been to this particular bar, where customers sit on a moving section that slowly revolves. "How unique," she cried, noticing the three piece combo off to the side, playing good dance music to a crowded floor. We had a couple of drinks and a few slow dances which were feeling very good.

After awhile we headed to her house in nearby Woodside. She invited me in for a drink or coffee. "I think coffee would be better," I answered.

We sit close on the couch enjoying small talk when, acting as one, we are in a passionate embrace. We make love on the couch and I am totally surprised by her unexpected torrential outburst, particularly considering her nun's background. A wave envelops us in a tight embrace that is warm, intimate and gratifying. We fall asleep in each others arms.

When we awake we shower together and head for her bed. With mutual passion, we make love again. It is Sunday. She has the day off and I have started my vacation. Who could ask for more!

We spend the rest of the day together. She makes a delicious breakfast of ham and eggs with English muffins. She loves pro-football (have I died and gone to heaven?) so we lounge and enjoy a leisurely afternoon.

"Can you get any time off during the next two weeks?" I ask, "because I'd like us to take a mini vacation somewhere. Could you suggest something you like?"

"Do you play golf?"

"I play at it, but I do like it," I answer.

"I used to play golf with my dad and have my own clubs, but it's been a while since I've played," She volunteers.

Almost immediately the ski town of Windham, New York comes to mind. With its beautiful, picturesque and not crowded golf courses and the fall foliage just starting, this would be a great get-away for a few days. I tell her about Windham Country Club with one of its holes overlooking the town and the church steeples jutting above the tree line and the mountains in the background. "It's just breathtaking to see."

She gives a delighted squeal and a little exuberant jump and tells me she has time coming to her which she can take.

We decide to go out for an early dinner since she has work in the morning.

Over our spaghetti and meatballs with Chianti, we talk of our mini vacation plans. After diner I drive her home and share a loving kiss before she gets out of the car. "I'll call you tomorrow," I whisper.

On the drive home to Long Beach, I'm feeling pretty happy and, as usual, the car lurches to the curb at The Saloon.

# Chapter 29

# MONDAY AT WAINWRIGHT HALL, LUNCH WITH MONIQUE

I HAD DECIDED THAT despite being on vacation I would work the next few Mondays evaluating the two Wainwright buildings.

Affable Jim Spencer, the fire safety director, is on the job early. We exchange routine information on his and my prospective jobs. I tell Jim I don't t believe there's enough work to sustain a full-time job but a periodic consulting inspection might be useful. I don't want to be just putting time in . . . besides, I think this whole thing is going to come to a head soon.

After my top-down inspection, I make note of a few minor violations and some areas of building deterioration. I notice a lot of loose mortar around the building's perimeter. I return to the roof and see some of the same conditions there. I'll check with Bob Park, the brother of firefighter Jim Park, who is a union bricklayer and will pump him on this condition for my report.

At noon I call Monique. She's ready for lunch. We meet in the lobby.

We head to Jackson's Hole, which features about twenty five ways to make a hamburger, my favorite being with Monterey Jack cheese smothered with mushrooms and onions with a side order of steak fries smothered in catsup. Monique says she's ravenous and orders the same.

"I'd like to run past you some suggestions for a lifestyle change," I tell Monique between bites. "The first thing is to change your residence . . . too many connections there. This is just like a person going to AA who has to change lifestyle," I begin.

I tell her of my friendship with a super who has many peers and possibilities for a new apartment. "But it will require some money under the table. Also, I've noticed you have a knack for decorating. Your apartment is very attractive, looks professionally done. I know the owner of Lenehan's Furniture Store and Warehouse on 72nd and Second Avenue and I'm sure I could get you a job there as a furniture salesperson. Maybe you'd be interested in interior design? Dan has several decorators working out of his place and with some training and experience I believe you could make a name for yourself."

"Gene, do you think I could really do that?" she looks at me with hope in her eyes.

"I'm sure of it! You kicked your drug and drinking habit which is much tougher than this so why not?!" She starts to cry and I put my arm around her to reassure her.

"I wish Yolanda was here," she says, "because I know with her help I could do it. You know, we had talked many times about me becoming a decorator. She thought I had a knack for it too."

"Monique, if you want it bad enough, it can be done."

We finish lunch. She tells me her stomach has started flip-flopping and she feels just like she did on her first day of high school, renewed and filled with anticipation.

"Just call me when you're ready and we can get the ball rolling." I make her promise, then walk her back to Wainwright Hall and head for Carlow's.

I'm on vacation and with the new developments of the past week, I have nothing better to do than to hang out a while at Carlow's, commiserating with Jim Hyland and waiting for the off-going 9x6 day tour to show up. I ask Jim if he's seen the super Jim Sullivan and he tells me he usually comes in around now. Sure enough, the super shows up and I fill him in with the particulars for securing an apartment for Monique who presently lives in Wainwright Hall. Unexpectedly, he erupts in anger. "Them bastard owners of Wainwright Hall and that Curzone House," he shouts, "they should be shot!" he roars in his thick Irish brogue. He then tells me that one of the original, fired supers in the previous old tenement, who was replaced by a harassment super, has a son who works for the FBI and knows that the management company is under investigation. "They'll get their comeuppance soon," he predicts. He calms down and asks me to let him know exactly where I'm looking for the apartment for Monique, adding that it should be no problem to find her a good one. As always, if you need something, want to know something, and you're in someone's confidence, it's amazing what you can find out.

Soon several of the men from the day tour arrive, the stories begin and I couldn't be happier. I head toward Long Beach about 9:00 p.m. and make my usual stop at The Saloon where Howard

Cosell's voice can be heard calling the Monday Night Football plays. There's a good crowd at the bar so I have a few beers and watch the game. About an hour and a half later, I head home and call Elizabeth and ask if she can get Thursday and Friday off this coming week.

"I'm sure I can but I'll check tomorrow," she says.

"I'm doing an inspection of Curzon House tomorrow," I tell her, "and should be home in the evening.

After Curzon House I repeat what I said last Monday at Wainwright Hall and the results are much the same. I confirm that there's not enough real work to sustain a full time position and will convey this to Dave Maier. I head home early to enjoy an evening walk on the beach and my favorite sunset dinner at Chauncey's, steak tidbits. Elizabeth calls to say she's gotten the days off, adding, "if possible, Bill Wilson would like a short 10 a,m. meeting with you next Wednesday at FBI Headquarters.

"Sounds good, I'll be there." Exhausted, I'm happy to be in bed early.

# Chapter 30

# DAVE MEETS DANNY O

THE FOLLOWING TUESDAY Monique calls to let me know that Dave had set up a meeting with Danny O through their contact, the super at the 86th Street. "They met at their usual location, a coffee shop on 88th and Third Avenue. As usual, there were no direct telephone contacts in their arrangement and Danny's services, as always, are being paid in cash: half down, the other half upon completion.

"Danny said Dave told him that he's tired of all the harassment actions and he's notified the affected supers on 80th Street that their services are no longer required. Dave's going to bring back legitimate supers, up the cash offers to the remaining tenants to move, or otherwise wait. With the rent controlled apartments operating at a loss they're still tax write-offs. He can't seem to look himself in the mirror and his stress level is causing severe depression, something cold blooded Danny O didn't begin to understand. Outside, he shook Danny's hand and walked away. Danny thinks that he can't trust that 'Jew bastard' anymore and considers what his next action will be.

"Two days later, at 86th Street, the super hears the story of one of the harassment supers, Danny tells me. When packing up to leave, he was confronted by the previous super who had been fired and lived across the street. 'Something must be happening to make you rats leave here,' the guy said to him. 'It was only a matter of time that the FBI would get you cruel bastards,' he added. Upon hearing this, the 86th Street super felt he had to get in touch with Danny O to find out if he knew what was going on. He calls Danny O and tells him to come to 86th Street immediately as he has heard some disturbing news.

"When Danny heard the news, he went into one of his deadly rages. 'I knew that bastard was up to something, he must be making a deal and he'll die before he gets away with it!' he says.

"So Danny hailed a cab and headed for the Colonial restaurant and asks the bartender if he's seen Sal Massetti lately and does be have his phone number. Sal Massetti is a connected soldier in the Leone family in Spanish Harlem who knows how to get 'things' done. Danny calls and gets Sal at home, asking Sal to meet him at the Colonial, 'I have a problem and wondered if you can help me out,' he explains to Sal, who agrees to meet him in an hour. When Massitti arrives, Danny fills him in with all the particulars of his problem.

'Through the grapevine I hear my business associate Wainwright Management is being investigated by the FBI This is street information and I hear you have a connection there and I would like to know if it's true. I could use your help,' Danny tells him. Sal confirms that he has a connection, a civilian employee who works in their legal department, and any official action goes through her. 'I don't use her unless it's important and she doesn't come cheap.' Sal says. Danny agrees to pay whatever it costs, and Sal says he'll get back to Danny as soon as he gets the information, if any.

"Three days later Sal calls Danny, confirming that Wainwright Management was indeed under investigation for arson and that this information would cost a thousand dollars. Danny is now seething, vowing to destroy that 'Mother Fucker' who's looking to make a deal for himself."

Monique is silent, finished with her report. I finish up the notes I've been furiously taking and thank her. I've got to move fast!

# Chapter 31

# THE FBI MEETING

THE NEXT MORNING I arrive at FBI Headquarters. Elizabeth meets me at the office door. Being the private person she is, I know she'll want to keep our new relationship on low profile. I'm all business.

After our greeting, Bill Wilson looks at me with a wry smile and asks, "Where the hell do you get your information from? The stuff you had on Danny O is extremely valuable and gives us an area to work on."

"I know the neighborhood well and know how to get information," I tell him. "Doormen, supers, mailmen and sanitation workers all have their hands on the pulse of the neighborhood. Street cops and fireman are other great sources, particularly if they were born and raised in the city and not in an isolated suburban bubble. I now have even more information for you, that I just learned yesterday," and I repeat Monique's conversation without mentioning her name. I watch their facial reaction and it tells me they are stunned. Finally bill says, "That info could come from anywhere, we have many civilian employees with low-level clearance. We'll start sniffing around, usually we connect."

"Sounds good, also my informant says that Danny O is becomming very suspicious of Dave Maier, he thinks Dave is going to make a deal with the FBI. He's angry and acting like a time bomb ready to go off! Am I correct that the way you got this case on Wainwright Management was through an FBI agent who was the son of a fired super"

Bill just blinked. Hoping to get a little more information, I ask how their investigation is going, "Does the FBI have a case strong enough to prosecute?" I ask. Vague as usual, Bill says there are still a lot of loose ends that they're hoping will all come together soon. They both thank me for my input and again warn me of possible dangers involved with my involvement.

It looks like I'm at a dead end for any more information but I ask, "Does the Agency ever brings suspects in for questioning prior to officially booking them like the NYPD does?"

"The procedure is similar. Why do you ask?" Bill wants to know.

"Do you know about Dave's service background in the army? He seems like a decent guy who you wouldn't expect to get caught up in a cowardly, greedy situation like this."

Bill shrugs. The meeting ends, Elizabeth walks me to the door and tells me she'll be in touch.

The door closes but I stand there for a while, lighting a cigarette. I hear their voices through the thin door.

"You've got a crush on him, don't you," Bill teases Elizabeth.

"Yeah right," is all Elizabeth can muster and I hear her rapid footsteps as she turns back to her office.

# Chapter 32

# TRIP TO WINDHAM MOUNTAIN

I'M REALLY ENJOYING vacationing, doing nothing on Long Beach, but I can't wait to pick up Elizabeth for our mini vacation. I leave just late enough Thursday morning to miss the traffic from Long Island and get to the city at 10:30. Elizabeth looks excited, tells me how much she's been looking forward to this trip. I opened the car door for her and watch her graceful moves into the car, her high heeled sandals showing off her pretty feet with painted toes. I'm a foot man. One of the first things I notice about a woman is her feet, particularly when they're connected to long attractive legs in sheer silk stockings, like Elizabeth's! My body movements get a little sporadic, which happens when I get turned on. I have difficulty inserting the key in the ignition, but she doesn't seem to notice.

On the New York State Thruway we get off at the Windham exit and head west on Route 23. The mid-October foliage is almost at its peak, a symphony of dazzling colors. After half an hour on the mountainous winding road we turn onto the "Brooklyn Bridge" at the beginning of the town and proceed to the Windham Mountain Inn, across the road from the great Windham golf course.

Jake Degan, from E 218 is part owner of the Inn and an ex-ski patrol member. We have our choice of the main house with dining room facilities or one of the motel units on the property. We chose the motel. Windham, is a ski town and the Mountain is one of the best, not too tough and great for families. But in the summer and fall its golf courses, restaurants and nature trails draw people willing to take the 120 mile drive from the City for the joy and comfort of an uncrowded paradise.

We enter the very cozy motel room with its spectacular view overlooking the golf course and a mountainous background with church steeples sticking up through the tops of the trees from the town below. I've brought the makings of a perfect martini — gin, vermouth, queen size green olives — and I make us two.

Sipping a martini and looking at Elizabeth with her legs crossed, looking over her glass into my eyes, brings on an excitement I can't control. I put down my drink and take her drink from her hand, lift her into my arms and kiss her. Her sensuous lips part and I explore her inviting mouth. Soon we are scrambling on the bed, ripping off each other's clothes.

Exhausted, we fall asleep in each other's arms. Hours later we wake and made love again, this time indulging in a slow, loving, exploring session. Finally Elizabeth takes a shower and I call the front desk to see if they can order us a pizza for delivery. I have more martinis ready when she returns, wrapped in a robe from the shower. The second martini always "levitates the brain above the usual Muck and Mire!"

Playing golf on an empty course on Friday afternoon was a delightful experience with Elizabeth. Whenever she got out of the golf cart for her shot I would get behind her, not able to keep my hands off her. On the secluded 17th hole, hitting off a high hill into a valley below, I hit a fortuitous hook into the pine needle-filled forest. As we were looking for my ball I pulled her gently down upon a soft bed of needles, laying my golf towel beneath her. "My father never told me golf could be this much fun," Elizabeth murmured, giggling with happiness We made love.

Two days of golf, dinner at romantic Vesuvios Restaurant on Friday night, Brandywine Restaurant on Saturday night, a ski-lift trip on Sunday to see the mountaintop foliage and plenty of loving in between made this a vacation I would not soon forget. The trip home on Sunday was easy driving since the highways are never too crowded this time of year.

On the drive home we chatted comfortably, like old friends, sharing more stories of our lives. We arrived in Woodside late Sunday afternoon and reluctantly said our goodbys. We held each other for a long time. Elizabeth whispered, "It couldn't have been a better time." I agreed. I watched as she entered her doorway, where she stopped and blew me a kiss.

# Chapter 33

# WHEN YOU PLAY WITH FIRE
# YOU CAN GET BURNED

EARLY MONDAY MORNING, my 38 snub-nosed Colt revolver in my side holster, I leave for Wainwright Hall. My plan is to stay at the firehouse tonight and tomorrow to go to the Police Pistol Range for some practice.

Arriving at 9:00 a.m., I do my usual inspection at Wainwright Hall, finish sooner than expected and write my reports. I call Monique, upstairs, but she isn't home. At 3:30 I get a call from Dave, saying that he'd like to meet with me at 5 o'clock in the Wainwright Hall office. With time to kill I decide to walk over to Carlow's for a little exercise, but first I give Monique a call upstairs. She is so excited I can hardly get a word in. "Calm down," I tell her.

"Gene, I've been trying to get in touch with you because I have important news."

"About what?"

"Danny O called an hour ago, said he's making his move back to Italy at the end of the month. He's getting rid of his furniture and apartment and taking an ocean liner — his dream — back to Italy. Then comes the kicker. He asks me if I want to go with him, tells me he's stashed enough money in Italy to live like a king for the rest of his life and if I want to come with him I'd never have to work again! The thought almost made me throw up, but I kept my cool and told him I've made new plans for a different life for myself but appreciated his offer. It's a good thing I didn't gag on that. He says the offer would remain on the table and if I change my mind to let him know. This slimy sonofabitch, just wants a gumada and a good lay. He sounded agitated, Gene, and I'm a little scared."

My adrenaline is pumping. I'm practically out of my seat. "I'm meeting with Dave in a little while. When we finish our business I'll get back to you as soon as possible."

"OK."

I decide to follow my initial plan for a walk and to think things out. I decide I must get in touch with the FBI immediately and at Carlow's I place a call and leave a message that I'll call back in a few hours with very important information. I have a couple of beers and head back for the meeting. I do not want to see this dirty bastard return to Italy. Many thoughts run through my mind. I get back to the office at 4:45. At 5 o'clock Dave shows up. He asks if everything is okay with today's inspection.

"It went well but Dave, I don't think there's enough work to sustain a full time job even with a third building in the future. Maybe a consultancy to do periodic exams of the buildings would work out better."

"Sounds good," he says. "I'll let you work out the schedule and then you can run it by me."

He asks if I want to go to Winters for a few drinks. "I have a few things on my mind that I'd like to discuss with you."

"Sure, but first I have to wash up a little." I walk past the file cabinets to a little hall and storage area leading to the bathroom. I'm just finishing up in the bathroom when I hear loud shouting from the office. I walk out and suddenly there is cursing and a shot fired, followed by a yell that sounded like Dave. I look over the file cabinets and there's this guy with a gun standing over Dave. He turns and sees me and yells, 'You must be that fucking fireman!'

I unholster my gun, drop to the floor and roll to the area between the files and entrance hall to the bathroom. From the floor I see him looking over the files for me. He turns and heads towards me. I fire one shot from the floor. He yelps and, with a startled look and eyes bulging, falls backward to the floor. I get up. The gun is out of his hand and there is no body movement. There's a blotch of blood showing in the middle of his chest. No sign of breathing. With shaking hands I lift his lifeless wrist to check for a pulse. None. Bubbles are coming from his mouth.

In a daze I check Dave and see a wound in his right shoulder. I call his name. He opens his eyes and whispers, 'Danny O shot me,' then passes out.

I call 911 and report a shooting. "What is your location and who's been shot?" the dispatcher asks. I give him the address, report that two men have been shot and both are unconscious. "I'm in a rear office leading to an under-ground garage. I'll be at the front door lobby of Wainwright Hall. I am an off duty fire captain and I'll have my badge showing on my jacket'"

150

I walk to the front lobby and I see two cops in a radio car screeching to a halt in front of the building. They burst in and ask what has happened.

"Two men are shot. Come on, I'll show you." I show them my gun on the file cabinet and run down what happened. My words are coming out erratically and I wonder if I'm making any sense.

They check Dave first, see he is still breathing and one of the cops gets on his portable radio asking if an ambulance is responding, which it is. They check Danny O and one exclaims, "I think this guy has bought the farm'" He's about to administer mouth to mouth when the ambulance arrives. The aides begin resuscitative efforts which last about ten minutes and then declare him D.O.A. The two cops now ask me to explain fully what has happened. I give the whole story again the best I can, then they start asking questions. 'Why were you here?' 'Where'd you get the gun?' 'What's your relationship to the two men?' "'Who shot who?'

I explain that I'm an ex-cop, have a pistol permit and that I work part time for this building management and that my boss is Dave Maier, who is the wounded person. "I don't know the second guy. All I know is that he burst in, cursed at Mr. Maier and shot him. When he saw me coming out of the bathroom, he cursed me and came after me with his gun. I shot him in self defense."

At this point two detectives arrive and the questioning begins all over again. The ambulance starts to remove Dave for a trip to the hospital and the medical examiner is called for the deceased. They tell me that they have to secure the crime scene and that they'll take me to the station for further questioning. As we leave we pass a TV unit taking as much footage as they can while shouting questions at me. The detectives tell them there will be a statement issued at the precinct as soon as they get the full details.

They take me to the 23rd Precinct on 103rd and Second Avenue which is also quartered with two fire units, L 43 and E 53.

I go over the whole story again, explaining that I am the Captain of Ladder Co. 13 on 85th Street. I'm asked again why I have a gun permit and I explain that when I left the police department to join the fire department I worked part time for the Pinkerton Agency, and that I had a permit because that doubled my salary. "I had the gun with me because I was going to stay at the fire house tonight and go to the Police Pistol Range in the morning."

That seemed to satisfy them. Just then Bill Wilson and Elizabeth Peters show up, flashing their agent credentials and informing the detectives that Wainwright Management and Dave Maier, the President, were under an FBI Arson investigation; that Dante Oderiono, the dead man, was suspected to be the arsonist who had actually set the fires. The agents know me because of the visit by Agent Peters to confiscate dead records of buildings that formerly stood on the sites of Wainwright Hall and the Curson House properties of Wainwright Management. Nobody asked the question I'd expected: how did I wind up working for him? If they had, I'd have told of our 'chance' meeting at Dave's penthouse birthday party.

After a conference between the FBI and the 23rd Precinct detectives it was concluded that my story was plausible and that I could leave after making a written statement — but to keep in touch for the expected follow up investigation. After giving my address and phone number, I tell them I'm on vacation leave and can be reached any time. When leaving the precinct I am deluged with questions from the TV crews. "Captain, what is your involvement in this?" They smell a story and as usual are relentless in pursuit.

Bill and Elizabeth offer to drive me to the firehouse where my car is parked. They tell the media there will be an official statement from both the police and the FBI, but no interviews will be given now. When we get in the car Bill asks if I want to stop awhile in order to settle down. Evidently, I'm showing the effects of the incident.

We stop for coffee and I realize I haven't eaten since breakfast That explains my nausea. We have sandwiches, kill about an hour and I decide to stick to my original plan. I'll stay at the firehouse overnight. It is almost 11 p.m. and I'm dog tired.

Luckily when we arrive at the firehouse, no media is around. The house watchman tells me the media were there but left a short while ago. I thank Bill and Elizabeth for their concern, say that I'll be in touch and head for the Battalion Office to inform the Chief of the incident. My friend, Battalion Chief, Tom Mannion, is on duty. When I enter his office he jumps up, gives me a hug and asks, "What the hell happened, Gene?"

"I'll tell you the whole story after I call my family. I'm sure they've already heard about it." He tells me to use his private phone.

My son answers the phone. He tells me that the shooting was all over the TV networks. He, his sister Mary and their mother, watched and knew from the story that I was okay, which I assure him is true. "I'll stay at the firehouse tonight and drive to Long Beach in the morning. And I'll call your sister Annie and tell her I'm okay."

Tom returns from the kitchen, where he'd gone to give me some privacy. After I tell him I'm staying in the firehouse overnight he brings out a bottle of brandy. I light up a cigarette and slowly tell him what happened tonight at Wainwright Hall. We talked for over an hour, and it was like medicine for me because in the telling I started shaking and breaking into a cold sweat. Finally exhausted, I lay down for a fitful sleep in the extra bed in my office.

I wake up early and ask the house watchman to tell any media that show up that I'd gone home. The incoming tour and members on duty knew what had happened. They were all in the kitchen early, concerned and asking if they could do any thing to help. My brothers . . . good guys. I filled them in on some details and am escorted to my car, which was pulled to the front of the firehouse for me. I head for Long Beach not knowing what to expect.

# Chapter 34

# THE AFTERMATH

DICK KEENAN IS at the door as I pull up. The October weather glistens with crisp bright blue skies. Dick, an old buddy from Engine 218 in Brooklyn, is as laid back as a person could get. He listens far more than he speaks, and he is a welcome sight.

"Gene, the phone's been ringing off the hook!" he says before I'm even out of the car. He hands me a note pad with a long list of names and phone numbers. "Your whole family called, frantic after seeing the news. I told them you were okay and were on your way home."

"Yeah. The news media. As always, they find ways to report news even before family members have been notified. That's why cops and firemen are not always happy to deal with them. Anything for a scoop!"

On the notepad I see that the Medical Office has called to

notify me that I am to be detailed to the Medical Office for light duty for thirty days, effective next Monday. Detective Koenig from the 23rd Precinct has also called requesting a follow-up interview, routine business to close up loose ends. There were more messages.

I put the list away and tell Dick that after a bite to eat I'm headed for a long walk on the beach and a therapeutic visit to Contemplation Rock to sort things out and to calm my mind. Friend that he is, Dick says he'll take the calls that are important or otherwise leave them on the answering machine.

I try to put in order the traumatic occurrences of the last two days as I walk the beach. My hands and body start to shake as what had happened or could have happened finally hits me. My façade has disappeared and now I have to begin dealing with it. All the hate for the arsonists seems to have drained from my body My first thought is of Marie Kale, the Fire Department therapist and counselor. I have to see her. When I go to the Medical Office on Monday, that will be my first order of business.

Two hours later when I return from the beach I call the 23rd Precinct, get Detective Koenig who wants to set up an appointment with me. He even offers to drive to Long Beach if I would find that more convenient. We decide tomorrow, Wednesday, at 11:00 a.m. would work. I thank him for his consideration and offer him directions. He tells me he is familiar with Long Beach and knows exactly where I am.

My firehouse calls to confirm my new detail to the Medical Office effective Monday and the Covering Officer on duty tells me that a woman named Monique had come to quarters several times and appeared very emotional asking how I was. "I couldn't give out your number, Cap, but told her I'd inform you of her visit."

He also tells me that the news media has been sniffing around about my whereabouts but were told "We have no information." There were also calls and visits from friends and members of the Fire Department, concerned with my welfare. "We told them all that you're okay but not able to return any calls at this time."

I thank the Covering Captain for his help and tell him that when things settle down I'll be in touch.

I decide to call Monique.

"Oh my God, Gene, what happened? I've been beside myself worrying about you," she gushes. "I haven't had a friend like you ever in my life! It's like having a brother who really cares about you."

I tell her I'm fine and that I'll come to see her when I get to my assignment next week. "We'll start making plans for you. Sometimes you need a catalyst in your life to make things happen, and this thing with Dave and Danny may be it." She's pleased when I give her my phone number and tell her to call me if she feels like it. I also give her the phone number of Jim Sullivan, the super, and mention that he'll be expecting her call about looking for an apartment around 72nd Street on the east side near the furniture factory and store. I also give her the number of the furniture store owner, so she can ask him about her job. "He's expecting your call. Don't worry, little sister, everything will be all right. This is one of those strange turns in life that may result in some good."

I spend the rest of the day screening calls and sleeping a lot and am surprised to be awaken by my three children who have come to see for themselves that I am okay! We have a nice visit. My daughter Annie has even brought food for a nice dinner she prepares for us.

The next morning at 11:00, Detectives Koenig and Moran from the 23rd Precinct show up for the interview. I go over the story again and they seem satisfied until Detective Koenig says, "Between the visit to Quarters from the FBI to obtain records, how did you get to know Dave Maier of Wainwright Management?"

I tell them of my meeting with Dave when my fire company responded to the smoke alarm arising from his birthday barbecue, and of his offer of a possible job. "Being curious about the whole situation, I decided to pursue it."

I sensed doubt in the two detectives and was relieved when Koenig replied that everything about the case was in order and to the best of their knowledge, I shouldn't be hearing from them again. I saved my sigh of relief for later. "The FBI has the case and we'll close it out that the incident was a case of self defense," Koenig stated as they got up to leave. The look in their eyes told me that even if they had some doubts, it served no purpose for the NYPD to pursue it.

Later that Wednesday afternoon, I watched the stories on the news which focused on the FBI investigation. I surmise that they must have made a statement to the press and that I just happened to be on the scene of a 'parting of the ways' of perpetrators of arson crimes for profit.

Agent Bill Wilson called, asking if I've seen the news reports of the shooting. I tell him I have, and mention my visit with the 23rd Precinct detectives this morning. "They appear to have accepted my account of self defense."

"We've made a public statement of the incident to the press along the same lines," Bill says. "We've also told the press about Dave Maier making a statement confessing to removing tenants

from old buildings with harassment, including arson, to effectu-
ate their plans." Bill further tells me that our bellicose Mayor, Ed
Koch, has made a statement to the real estate industry that any
further incidents will be prosecuted and "people will go to jail."
I'm glad to hear this. He says he and Elizabeth would like to get
together with me again. I tell him of my detail to the Medical
Office starting Monday and that anytime next week would be
okay. He asks me to call him on Monday to set up a meeting with
them. "Elizabeth would like to hear from you as soon as you get
a chance," he says. I figure she's told Bill about our relationship,
which makes me feel very good.

Over the weekend I started getting back into my routine. I
stopped by The Saloon a couple of times, running into friends
and other firemen. No one seemed pushy about exact details,
only wanting to make sure that I'm okay. With the visits from my
children and friends, things are gradually returning to normal.
Despite my unexpected bad dreams about the shooting, I managed to get some rest and made a mental note to go over all this
with Marie Kale at our meeting.

Saturday I get another call from the firehouse, from my friend
Lt. Jerry Guilfoyle. After filling him in with some of the details
we make plans to see each other next week, when I'll tell him
the whole story. He's already aware of my detail next week.
"Gene, I got a visit to the firehouse from Dave Maier's brother.
He's asking if it's possible for you to go see Dave at the hospital .
. . something about his brother being indebted to you for saving
his life and he'd be grateful if you could get to see him." Jerry
gives me the brother's phone number.

# Chapter 35

# THE TRUTH ABOUT DAVE

I GET DAVE'S BROTHER'S wife on the phone. She excitedly calls her husband to the phone.

Dave's brother introduces himself as Sid, and tells me how grateful he is that I saved his brother's life. Dave wants to see me, Sid says, to thank me personally and Sid's already cleared this with the FBI if I agree to the visit. "Agent Wilson would like you to call him so he can give approval for the visit to the guards."

Sid is a bundle of emotion as he continues: "I love my brother and despite what it seems, he's a good guy. He's always been good to his family and friends, does favors for colleagues, and makes generous donations to local charities. He's a hard worker, a builder, and these three buildings are his most shining accomplishment. He just got caught up."

I like Sid instantly. "No need to apologize for Dave," I tell him. "I already knew that he's intrinsically a decent man. We all can make mistakes," I tell him. "I'll contact Agent Wilson about seeing Dave." I hear a sob.

"Thanks, I don't know how to repay you."

Bill is out when I call so I leave a message. An hour later Bill calls and I tell him about my conversation with Dave Maier's brother and how I'd like to visit Dave at Lennox Hill Hospital. Bill says, "Okay, I'll arrange it for Tuesday evening after five o'clock." I thank him for his help and tell him I'll talk with him on Monday as planned.

Sunday morning I put in a call to Elizabeth with some trepidation because I don't know how she's reacting to Monday's episode. She's not home and I leave a message that I'll be home all day. When she calls back I can hear the tightness in her voice. I brace myself, not knowing what to expect.

Elizabeth is all business. "Under the circumstances Bill, who knows of our relationship, doesn't think we should see each other for awhile to avoid arousing suspicion."

"I have a 30-day detail to the Medial Office and agree that distance is a good idea during this period."

Silence!

Now her voice becomes mellow and she starts to tell me how she'll never forget the acute fear she felt when she got the call to respond to a double shooting at Wainwright Hall. She envisioned me dead, sprawled on the floor, blood all around me. Frankly, the more I think about the life and death danger of my scheme, the less sure I am that I did the right thing. "I have to calm myself down, Gene, to see where these feelings go."

Sadly I tell her I understand, "This has been an unusual and difficult situation and I hope time will be on our side. Please keep in touch Elizabeth," I say, trying not to sound too upset. "I need you."

She says she will be in touch and we hang up.

On Tuesday evening I drive up to the hospital, making my way through the rush hour traffic. In the lobby I find out the floor Dave's on and check in at the nurse's station when I get there. The nurse tells me I've got to talk to the agent who's guarding Mr. Maier and she directs me to the prisoner holding area. I introduce myself to the FBI agent, show him my identification and he tells me it's okay to go in.

Dave, not looking too worse for wear, smiles, grasps my hand and thanks me for coming. "I just want you to know how damned grateful I am to you, not for just saving my life, but for far more important reasons. Somehow you showed up in my life — I don't question how or why but you found me at my lowest moral point, and you've helped me get my life back to where it was when I felt good about what I was doing."

I'm taken aback but Dave, still holding my hand, continues:

"When I was young I was very proud of my family for overcoming setbacks in their lives with hard work, integrity and honesty. I always relied on those principles which made me strong and confident and clear-headed. I look with pride on my war service to my country, but in the last several years . . . I don't know what happened to that person. Greed and power changed me into a person I've come to hate. There was a lot of money at stake and I didn't want to lose. I agreed to things I shouldn't have and then I became a part of the evil world I knew existed. Meeting you triggered some deep feelings. I felt unclean, dirty and disgusted with myself. I prayed for a way to feel good again.

"Being shot and nearly killed offered me a way to redeem my soul. I've made a full statement to the FBI, and want to accept my punishment. Maybe then I'll get that old feeling back and regain my family's faith in me! And Gene, I want you to respect me for who I really am and not for what I've become." He started to cry.

I put my hands gently on his shoulders. "Commander, you already have and your 'tank' is back on course. Your family is behind you and your guilt will fade. No one should judge you. After all, don't forget that seventy percent is a passing grade." His smile was grateful. "I'll keep in touch, if I can be of any help."

I left the hospital knowing that Dave had bared his soul and that the cleansing process had begun. On the drive back to Long Beach I felt very peaceful and knew that things were going to be good for Dave and his family.

# Chapter 36

# LIGHT DUTY AT THE MEDICAL OFFICE

I REPORT AT 9:00 a.m. at the downtown Medical Office, a large building that houses two active fire companies in addition to the fire department ambulances and doctor's cars. The four floors above contain offices where ambulatory sick members must report for an exam by department doctors. The Medical Office treats all medical leaves and keeps all medical records of department members. It has a staff of at least fifteen doctors, in all specialties, and is always a beehive of activity.

After many greetings with former company members from previous assignments, it turned out to be like old home week with firemen from all over the city. Most of the men there had heard of the shooting incident. The network of firemen, even though numbering 10,000 is like a family.

They assign me to the light duty desk where the Officers in Charge assign firemen to various light jobs such as clerical positions in offices throughout the fire department or assignments as Chief and ambulance drivers, or as guards in firehouses in bad neighborhoods so that someone is always present when the fire trucks are out on alarms.

Officer light duty jobs (mostly clerical) are also assigned at this desk. These are jobs with flexible hours, to be shared with a few other officers temporarily assigned there. That's where I'm assigned. My first thought is to make an appointment to see Marie Kales. I leave her a message and the extension where I can be reached. She calls mid-morning and I tell her I think I could use some help in talking things out. Marie tells me she is at her other office, the counseling unit in the fire boat administrative building at Battery Park, and could see me at 1:00 p.m.

I take the subway to Battery Park and walk over to the old building which is now an official landmark. Two huge fire boats sit on both sides of the building. She greets me with a huge hug and kiss and tells me that it was she who recommended the thirty day detail in order to remove me from media access and public involvement. I know her brother, Ed Smyth, a fellow captain from Brooklyn. He had already called me, concerned.

"A trauma of this magnitude has more repercussions than you would think and I'm so glad you've come to see me," Marie begins.

We talk at length. I tell her the whole story and this plus her explanations make me feel much better. I see why she had the reputation of helping brother firemen through crisis. Her big hug and kiss were also welcome.

Her first question: how much guilt did I feel? Despite this guy being sub-human to me for causing suffering and possible death to the older tenants in buildings he had set on fire, I was still surprised that my reaction included remorse over the taking of a life. I knew in Korea that our weapons had killed enemy soldiers but I had never shot one as up close as I'd shot the arsonist.

"It's a natural feeling when seeing the death of a once living person. It will take time for it to pass. I recommend that you take an anti-depressant to help you through. I'll give you something and you come and see me next week."

When I got back to the Medical Office I called Bill Wilson and we arranged for a meeting Wednesday, the day after tomorrow. I had the leeway to do anything that came up, so getting Wednesday afternoon off was no problem. After my meeting with Bill, I plan to run up and see Monique if she's home.

Wednesday afternoon, I drive to FBI Headquarters on 72nd Street. Bill greets me at the door and tells me that Elizabeth had other department business and sends her regards. Bill goes over his conversations with Dave and his willingness to come clean on all his illegal activities.

"I can see what you meant about him being a decent guy just caught up in bad stuff. It almost seems like an act of purification. Since he's very active in real estate associations he'll make an off-the-record recommendation to them to cease and desist because of the consequences sure to come to them."

Bill says the case has been just about completed and that he is also convinced that Dave was the only person in Wainwright Management who was involved, which I agree with. He also thanks me for all the information I had supplied, saying that the case would be nowhere near this point without it.

"In spite of this, I can't be more vehement in what I think of your involvement. It wasn't especially wise to be personally dealing with the likes of a dangerous criminal like Danny O. This could have very easily come to a bad conclusion."

I had to agree with him 100 percent: I'd operated with emotion instead of logic. I planned to take his sound advice.

"One thing I will tell you is that you would have made a good FBI agent with your knowledge of the inner City and your various sources of information." He also told me that Elizabeth was very upset and traumatized over the incident. I left Bill's office hoping our paths would someday cross again under better circumstances.

I drive uptown after calling Monique. She'll be meeting me at the Jackson Hole in twenty minutes. I get there first and take a table in the rear for privacy. She arrives shortly and gushes, "How did you ever keep from getting killed by that dangerous and evil man? I was afraid for my life whenever I was around Danny O!"

"I guess my police and army training kicked in, and luckily I survived." We order great big juicy hamburgers with all the toppings. She tells me the good news that Jim Sullivan called her and said there would be no problem getting her an apartment near 72nd Street. He mentioned how much money would be needed for the Super besides the required two months security. Tomorrow they were going to look at a few apartments. She had also contacted Don Lenahan at the furniture store, who told her to come in any time during business hours.

"I'm so excited about these changes in my life that I never thought could happen. It would've been impossible without you, Gene. Why have you been so good to me"?

"Because I like you," I answered, "and besides, Yolanda told me you had a heart of gold and are a diamond in the rough, and I agree with her."

After eating, I told Monique about my thirty day assignment to the medical office. "I'll keep in touch and the next time I see you I hope everything will have fallen into place. Call me if you need me."

That night I call Elizabeth. "I think I have finally started to settle down and unwind from the effects of the shooting."

She wishes she could see me but thinks that Bill's advice is sound. "The case against Wainwright Management and Dave Maier is going well, particularly with his confession. Dave's lawyer is looking for a plea bargain which we believe can be worked out. The Agency is pleased and we're getting a lot of 'attaboys' from other agents and our bosses. Being a female agent can be hard at times and the recognition is very gratifying." She also wonders what her next assignment will be. I tell her that I'll keep in touch and hope we can be together soon.

"Me too!" she says.

# Chapter 37

## BACK TO THE FIRE HOUSE

TWO WEEKS AT the Medical Office has been dull and I'm going nuts. My two subsequent meetings with Marie Kale went well. I decided against medication because I felt good and didn't want it to prevent my return to full duty. I couldn't wait to get back to the fire house and to see Elizabeth as soon as possible. I've never been good on the phone and our relationship now seemed vague and distant. I wondered if the shooting had had any effect.

When I see Marie again I tell her I'm fine and dying to get back to work and normalcy.

"I'll put you back to full duty at the end of the week.."

"Thanks, Marie, I can always count on you to come through. My best regards to your brother. Tell him I'm fine and I'll keep in touch."

I notify the Third Division that I'm back to full duty effective

Friday. They in turn notify Ladder 13 and the 10th Battalion, the normal procedure. I check with the firehouse, and they tell me all is back to normal: the media hasn't been around. Evidently this is an old story already. I leave a message with Elizabeth about my discontinued detail, and ask if she'd like to get together on Saturday for a nice dinner in Manhattan.

\* \* \*

Elizabeth calls that evening and tells me Saturday's fine and that she'd like to go back to Sans Gullotte. Her tone is friendly but still formal, so I can't tell what Saturday will be like.

But when I pick her up Saturday, she abandons restrain and jumps into my arms. The emotional clouds from the shooting are lifting. She feels good again and I'm overjoyed with her display of affection.

Dinner is delightful. We stay a little longer than planned and are both pleasantly cocktailed for the ride to Woodside. I'm extra careful because of the drinks and appreciate my cushion of knowing many of the cops en route. Elizabeth skips into her house bare footed which turns me on and we make love on her living room couch with total abandonment. Torrents of pleasure pass between us and the closeness of her velvety smooth body under mine takes my breath away.

As my breathing is returning to normal, Elizabeth says, "I'd like to go to Long Beach with you, see your Contemplation Rock and walk the beach the way I used to at Far Rockaway Beach as a kid. My family always had a summer bungalow there."

"I'd love to introduce you to my rock. I'll be off next weekend. We can do it then."

"Sounds great! I can get off on Friday and I'd like so much to see the places you always talk about."

"Okay, I'll pick you up Friday morning."

# Chapter 38

# BACK TO FULL DUTY

SUNDAY MORNING I head for the firehouse from Elizabeth's. It feels great to get back to work. I love the closeness of my brothers in the firehouse. They tell me that the news media occasionally calls, asking of my whereabouts, if I'm still on special assignment and when I'm expected back.

Jerry Guilfoyle greets me like a long lost brother. We have coffee in the kitchen with the rest of the off-going and incoming crews. Naturally there are many questions and I tell the story that has been reported. Later when it is no longer news, or no longer has the possibility of having any effect, I'll tell them the truth. Jerry Guilfoyle, who knows all the circumstances, keeps a straight face as I answer all the questions. They eventually stop and I feel a gradual return to normal conversations.

Sunday has no business activities except for an outdoor drill with apparatus training at 11:00 a.m. Some of the new men are anxious to operate the Tower Ladder and this is their time to play with their big toy under the watchful eyes of the senior men. That is how my first captain in Long Island City made us relax. "Just take the apparatus up and down the huge piers by yourselves until you get comfortable." Not the usual training procedure but it gives the men the confidence and relaxation needed. No pressure; just play with it. Often I think of my old captain, Tom Lynch, and marvel at the way he always brought out the best in us.

I bring my men to a large sanitation depot on 96th and the East River, used for loading garbage barges, Here they can maneuver the fire trucks and become familiar without having to worry about hitting other vehicles.

On the way back from drill we get an alarm for a fire at 91st and 2nd Avenue. It turns out to be a man who fell asleep in bed with a cigarette, causing his mattress to smolder and soon ignite. We put the fire out with two hand extinguishers and lifted the victim off the floor, where most victims of this type fire are found, and removed him to another room. He appeared drunk and unable to stand. This is typical of carbon monoxide poisoning, the result of incomplete combustion, particularly with a smoldering mattress. It completely disorients the victim and causes arm and leg paralysis. When trying to get out of bed, the victim falls to the floor and can't move. In a short while the man recovered his mobility and no longer appeared drunk. Now he felt embarrassed but thankful to us for saving his life. This is a classic example of why smoking in bed is one of the biggest causes of fire fatalities.

The rest of the Sunday is great, a good lunch and a New York Giants-Washington Redskins football game on television, intermingled with a false alarm run and another run for an electrical emergency. Sunday is usually the firemen's perfect day in the fire-house, but we keep this little secret to ourselves.

After work I stop at Carlows with a few off-going men. An Irish band is playing and the dance floor is full. This is the local weekend crowd, a lot of service people — doormen, supers, off duty cops and firemen, restaurant workers and cooks, mostly all Irish — and they know the beat of the neighborhood. Jim Sullivan walks over, grabs my hand and pulls me close with the other. "Man, I'm sure glad that nothing happened to you," he says in a nice Irish brogue. "I've taken care of your lady friend and it looks as if she likes an apartment on 71st and York Avenue, a nice block."

"I appreciate what you've done, Jim, and I know she appreci-ates it. She's had a tough life."

"Anytime, Captain."

I tell everyone I like to be called Gene but they seem to like calling me captain.

Irish people, particularly first generation Americans, have an affinity for civil service jobs since they are usually their first step into the mainstream. They're fun and generous people. After an enjoyable two hours I enjoy the trip back to Long Beach and my next favorite stop, The Saloon. This time I obey my car's auto-matic reaction. The regulars plus a few firemen makes for a big greeting when I enter. I appreciate this first day of a return to normalcy. A couple of city cops come over, are brief with warm well wishes, glad I'm okay and someday I'm sure we'll go over the whole story as it really happened.

My roommate Dick Keenan is also there. I'm starved and suggest we sit in the back restaurant. We grab a table and enjoy a great big juicy hamburgers and steak fries, which The Saloon is noted for, and a few more beers. Near 11:00 we go home. I'm looking forward to a good night's sleep for tomorrow's day tour.

Next day, Monday, we have Apparatus Field Inspection Duty and I decide to take the apparatus to Wainwright Hall so I can show the men the scene of the shooting, which they're all curious about. Jim Spencer is in his office. When he sees me he jumps off the chair and gives me a huge embrace. "Am I ever glad to see you! Is everything okay?"

"Yeah, I'm fine. Needed a rest from the shooting so the Department detailed me to the Medical Office."

"I just can't believe what happened," he says, " I went to see Dave and he sure feels indebted to you. He told me he hasn't felt this clean in a long time and even apologized to me for his behavior. I like him, Gene, always have, and I hope he can work through this. It's like a huge black cloud has lifted. He's willing to pay his dues and I know he'll make it back. Can I tell Dave's brother about this visit?"

"That would be fine. Give my regards to his family." I leave, with Jim and I promising to keep in touch.

On my arrival Wednesday for the night tour I get a surprise. Awaiting me is a letter from Yolanda. She's seen the news accounts of the shooting, can't believe the developments and wants to hear from me. She gives me her number in Fort Chaffee, Arkansas, and asks that I please call her one evening as soon as possible, because she's anxious to hear my side of the story. 'I can't believe you were able to kill Danny O, you are one lucky person because he was a deadly and feared person. No one screwed with him.'

I call Monique and give her this latest news from Yolanda and the basic contents of the letter. Monique asks me for Yolanda's phone number. I give it to her, knowing that Yolanda would love to hear from Monique and learn about the positive changes that are starting to happen in her life. "Tell Yolanda I can't call the next two nights from the firehouse, but give her all the particulars and tell her I'll call her Friday night from Long Beach."

# Chapter 39

# NEWS FROM ELIZABETH

I PICK UP ELIZABETH in Woodside after finishing my night tour on Friday morning and we drive to Long Beach. Indian summer has kicked in. It's a beautiful, sunny and unseasonably warm fall day. I make her breakfast in Dick's bungalow, which is about 100 yards from the beach, then we change clothes, grab beach towels and a couple of beers, and head for a day at the beach.

We set up just a short distance from my Contemplation Rock, and after getting organized we walk to it. We dangle our feet in the shallow incoming tide. The day is perfect and Elizabeth just loves it. The rock is big enough for two people to lie on and I show her how we both fit. She seems in a quiet, reflective mood. I figure that whatever is on her mind will come out when she's ready.

We sunbathe the whole afternoon, have a few beers, nap and

lazily pass the time talking and laughing. Late afternoon, with the tide now at low ebb, we walk several miles on the flat beach. There are eight big stone jetties to the mile; we walk ten there and ten back, about two and a half miles. It's now almost time for the sun to set and we're in no rush. We sit on 'my' rock to enjoy the array of orange, pink and lavender against a blue sky containing white wispy ribbons of clouds. A purple tint is given to the ocean. As the sun goes down, Elizabeth becomes quiet, pensive.

"Gene, I have something to tell you. Since the Wainwright case is finished, I've been asked to take an assignment undercover as a teacher in a school district that's under heavy investigation for irregularities and possible child molestation. I can't give you any details and I don't know how long I'll be undercover and unable to contact you. Usually the assignments are no longer than six months — most are shorter but occasionally they take more time. It's difficult for me to tell you this because your coming into my life has been wonderful, but this is my career."

It felt as if I've been slam dunked in the stomach. Our relationship has been one of deep caring and pleasure for me and this unexpected development is thoroughly not welcomed. "I know I have no control or say in this matter, but I want you to know that I'll be here for you when you finish your assignment. My feelings for you won't change in any way from what I feel now."

We look into each others eyes and share a soft, loving kiss. We sit on the rock for quite a while, saying nothing, just holding hands.

We walk back to the bungalow and Dick is there after finishing a day tour at his firehouse in Brooklyn. He's on his way up to The Saloon for a few beers. Friday night is always busy.

"After we shower, we'll meet you there for a few drinks, then we're going to Lenny's for a nice sit-down dinner."

"Sounds good, see you later," Dick says, as he walks out the door.

Elizabeth and I make love more tenderly than passionately. "Don't worry, Elizabeth, what's meant to be will be. All I know is that I'm madly in love with you and always will be."

A while later we shower and dress and head for The Saloon where I hope a few cocktails will lighten our mood.

The Saloon crowd is huge and soon puts us in a festive mood. All who meet Elizabeth like her immediately. After a couple of drinks we walk the few blocks to Lenny's Steakhouse. We enjoy big juicy steaks and probably a few more drinks than we should have. Our path back to the bungalow is slightly irregular. We fall into a somewhat fretful sleep.

After a lazy morning and a late brunch, we prepare to enjoy another day in Long Beach. The showcase of Long Beach is our two and a half mile boardwalk which is just perfect for biking. I had borrowed a girl's bike for Elizabeth from one of our neighbors and we spent a good deal of the afternoon riding the boardwalk and sitting on the benches enjoying the sun and the beautiful ocean view. We stopped at one of the concessions for double scoop cones of Rum Raisin ice cream.

A concert on the beach at the West End of the Boardwalk was planned for the evening. We go back to the bungalow for some lovemaking, shower and walk to the concert. On the way we stop for slices of pizza and beer.

The concert was great, we small talk on the way back and stop again at Lenny's for a nightcap with my favorite Long Beach bartender, Vincent, a tall black southern gentleman who has captivated most of the Long Beach patrons. Back at the bungalow, Elizabeth asks if it's okay for us to leave Sunday morning as she would like to start organizing for her new assignment. "I have to set up a new residence to be ready for the January start of classes."

I tell her it would be fine and we head for the bedroom to make love for what might have to hold us for a very long time. It is bittersweet. I try to remember all the little nuances of her body and how she feels under my touch.

Our ride to Woodside the next morning is quiet. I tell her again how much I care for her and she tells me of her feelings for me. I see small tears in the corners of her eyes, I know it isn't easy for her either. I reach in my pocket for some change and tell her I am only a phone call away.

At her door I hold on to her. I kiss her warm subdued mouth and the tears that are slowly sliding down her cheeks, then turn from her and leave. I couldn't take much more without breaking up emotionally. All I can hope for is that I will see her again. I look back at her from my car. She gives a small wave and blows a kiss with glistening eyes. I wave back and drive away.

\* \* \*

Back at Long Beach, I sink into a chair and wipe my eyes. I'm thinking about going on a bender when I remember that I was supposed to call Yolanda Friday night. I call her number in Fort Chaffee and luckily reach her home.

"Gene! I don't know where to start, I'm so glad to be in touch again — especially with the good things that are happening to Monique."

I go through the whole story of the shooting. I tell Yolanda that besides her information about Danny's involvement with the Wainwright arsons, Monique supplied me with Danny's identity and his address, which I passed on to the FBI investigators. Yolanda remembered the female FBI agent coming to the fire-house for fire records of the previous buildings on the new hi-rise site, and now she realized that it was my involvement with the FBI that helped to undo the case against Danny and Wainwright.

"Danny sought revenge against Dave thinking he'd been the FBI informant," Yolanda exclaimed, the whole picture coming together for her now. We talked for at least an hour, I didn't mention my involvement with Elizabeth as that could complicate things more. Yolanda told me about her new assignment of helping translate the interviews with the Boat People who had arrived recently from Cuba. "They're looking for any spies that could have been among them," she says. "As soon as this assignment is over, which will be soon, I'm returning to New York, the only place I'm truly happy."

We both agree that we'll keep in touch with Monique.

The conversation with Yolanda had taken my mind off my sad feelings, but only temporarily. My head spins when I think of all that's happened in the last five months. Where do I go from here? I have no clue. I think it's going to be a long lonely winter.

# Chapter 40

# ENDINGS AND BEGINNINGS

ONE EVENING IN mid-April, returning to Long Beach from the first of my two day tours, I checked my phone messages and see a message from a John Peters, Elizabeth's father! I couldn't believe it. I'd never met the man and I haven't heard from Elizabeth since she left for her undercover assignment. I was hoping her assignment was nearing an end and that I'd be hearing from her soon. I've been missing her terribly, and the sweet breezes of spring aren't helping me forget.

His message says he is staying at the Hilton Hotel in Manhattan and would I please return his call. I call the number and John Peters, a retired cop, answers the phone.

"Any chance I could meet you in New York City? I'd like to talk to you."

I tell him of course, that I could meet him at the Hilton tomorrow night at 7:00 o'clock. He says he'll be waiting at the piano bar.

The last five months have been an adjustment period for me and I'm finally starting to snap out of my doldrums. Some positive things have happened: Monique has made a great transition, loves her new job and new apartment and her boss, Don Lenehan, is very pleased with her. He's told her she should go to an interior decorating school because she has a definite talent. She's begun making arrangements to attend a school on Manhattan's West Side.

Yolanda returned to New York and lives in Jackson Heights, Queens. She's taking a crack at writing another book. She and Monique have become very close. The both of them met up with me on St. Patrick's Day and we had a ball. They still love firemen! Dave Maier received a three to five year sentence after his plea bargain and is handling it very well. He and his family have kept in touch, which I feel very good about. I visited with him once and hope to go again.

After my day tour I take the downtown Lexington Avenue Subway to 57th Street: traffic would be murder at this time of day. I walk to the Hilton and head for the bar lounge where I see an elderly, civil service type gentleman giving me a wave. I know this is Elizabeth's father. After our initial greeting we go through our backgrounds, his as a policeman and mine as a fireman: we have a common bond.

He gets serious and says, "I probably have no business getting into something I know little about, but I have to get a few things off my chest. What did Elizabeth tell you about going undercover? What were the circumstances?"

"All I know, John, is that she'd received a covert assignment and couldn't tell me about it and that she had to leave almost immediately. I'm not complaining in any way — I know her job entails these types of assignments but I had to suck up all the wonderful feelings I have about your daughter and how much I've missed her. What else could I do? I only hope that someday very soon we can be together again. Have you heard from her lately? How is she doing?"

"She's fine, Gene, but she isn't on an undercover assignment. She's living with me in Harrisburg, Pennsylvania where she was transferred by her own request."

He has my full attention now, but I'm speechless waiting for him to explain.

"Here's the whole story. I'm protestant, was married to a wonderful religious Irish Catholic woman. She always wanted Elizabeth to be a nun and I figured if that's what they both wanted, how could I interfere, even though she was my only child and I would've loved grandkids. When my wife died, Elizabeth was fourteen years old and knew what her mother wanted for her. After graduating from high school, she entered the convent. But after a lot of soul searching, she realized it wasn't meant for her. After eight years, she came out of the Order.

"She wanted me to have my grandkids but couldn't seem to find a husband and have a family. Five years ago she was accepted by the FBI and became an agent. She loved the work and at the same time hoped to eventually get married and give me the grandchild she knew I had wanted. But five years went by and she felt that time was becoming a huge factor. So she decided she was going to get pregnant by a man she'd pick out and interview, which she did. This is where you came into her life. She didn't know, however, that she was going to fall in love with you."

An explosion goes off in my head. I'm grinning now.

"Gene it's breaking my heart to see how unhappy she is and how she misses you, though under the circumstances she couldn't tell you. I'm only a desperate father who loves his daughter and it's killing me to see her like this, maybe even unhealthy. I have no right to tell you these things or expect anything from you, but I had to talk to you and let you know how things really are."

"When and how are you going back to Harrisburg?" I ask.

"I catch a train tomorrow at noon."

"Cancel it. We're driving back together, tomorrow."

# AFTERWORD

THERE ARE TWISTS of nonfiction woven throughout this story. All the fireman stories are true, using the men's real names, which is what they wanted. The records of arson fires were from an investigation into the use of tenant coercion to force them out.

The love story was taken from an actual firehouse visit by an FBI agent who was an ex-nun. I tried to get information on the FBI investigation but was unsuccessful, despite my Freedom of Information Act inquiries and my research on the internet. The only real proof came from the knowledge of victimized tenants, doormen and superintendents of the buildings involved, and word on the street.

Information on the arsonist was real but unprovable from my sources, mainly the now-fictionalized Yolanda.

Greg Stajk, my probie, was killed at the World Trade Center twenty years after this story occurred. In 2007 I met Greg's mother, Marge, at a Fire Department Mass for our lost brothers.

I told her about writing this book that was dedicated to her son. She asked to read my galley copy and, when she returned it, she also gave me several photos of Greg and our championship softball team. I was moved, particularly by the photo of Greg with Victor the Constrictor wrapped around his shoulders.

Years do not change the feelings firemen had for each other during those painful but golden years. The young men who followed us and were killed at the World Trade Center became part of our legacy. They are men who will not be forgotten. The devotion to the job, to brother firefighters and the fun we shared, some say, will bring us all together again for our next softball championship.

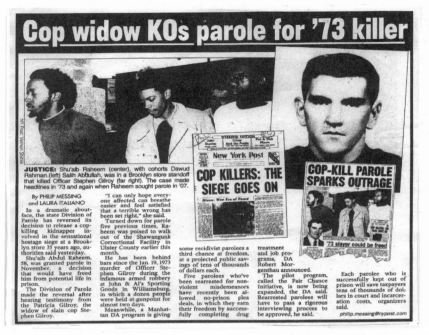

## Cop widow KOs parole for '73 killer

**JUSTICE:** Shu'aib Raheem (center), with cohorts Dawud Rahman (left) Salih Abdullah, was in a Brooklyn store standoff that killed Officer Stephen Gilroy (far right). The case made headlines in '73 and again when Raheem sought parole in '07.

**New York Post**

**COP KILLERS: THE SIEGE GOES ON**

**COP-KILL PAROLE SPARKS OUTRAGE**

'73 slayer could be freed

By PHILIP MESSING and LAURA ITALIANO

In a dramatic about-face, the state Division of Parole has reversed its decision to release a cop-killing kidnapper involved in the sensational hostage siege at a Brooklyn store 35 years ago, authorities said yesterday.

Shu'aib Abdul Raheem, 58, was granted parole in November, a decision that would have freed him from potential life in prison.

The Division of Parole made the reversal after hearing testimony from the Patricia Gilroy, the widow of slain cop Stephen Gilroy.

"I can only hope everyone affected can breathe easier and feel satisfied that a terrible wrong has been set right," she said.

Turned down for parole five previous times, Raheem was poised to walk out of the Shawangunk Correctional Facility in Ulster County earlier this month.

He has been behind bars since the Jan. 19, 1973 murder of Officer Stephen Gilroy during the infamous armed robbery at John & Al's Sporting Goods in Williamsburg, in which a dozen people were held at gunpoint for almost two days.

Meanwhile, a Manhattan DA program is giving some recidivist parolees a third chance at freedom, at a projected public savings of tens of thousands of dollars each.

Five parolees who've been rearrested for nonviolent misdemeanors have recently been allowed no-prison plea deals, in which they earn their freedom by successfully completing drug treatment and job programs, DA Robert Morgenthau announced.

The pilot program, called the Fair Chance Initiative, is now being expanded, the DA said. Rearrested parolees will have to pass a rigorous interviewing process to be approved, he said.

Each parolee who is successfully kept out of prison will save taxpayers tens of thousands of dollars in court and incarceration costs, organizers said.

philip.messing@nypost.com

*Denial of parole for the killers of the cop at the 1973 shootout at John-Al's Sporting Goods store.*